© Mark Kotting

Nappy Rash

© *All copyrights remain with the author*

First Edition

ISBN 1-903110-16-5

Cover Design by Owen Benwell

Published in 2005 by
Wrecking Ball Press
24 Cavendish Square, Hull, HU3 1SS

Mark Kotting

Nappy Rash

For Trace, for everything

Chapter 1

All I've got to show for my thirty eight years is the hand I'm holding, and a green medallion swinging from my neck with a taxi driver's number stamped on. I'm allowed in some bus lanes, not in others. Where's the sense in that? And who cares? I fucking do.

Someone's figured it out, on a computer in some office, tucked behind his desk. All sorted. Putting in a set of lights here, a roundabout there. My point? It's a fucking mess.

I don't trust anyone. I used to. I thought l could read sets of eyes. Not now. I mean, who the fuck can? But as I said, I thought I could. Now I couldn't tell a good man from a bad man. A chump from a champ.

Only yesterday a carpenter flagged me. He didn't have long hair, or look like Jesus. I should have known. It was one in the morning, no traffic, we were bouncing along. He's telling me about his job, about him. Talking, we call it. His mates work at Tesco's, in blue check shirts. That's not for him, swiping frozen chickens across scanners, dead skin, packed in plastic. He's a carpenter, a working man, cuts wood like the best of them. He wasn't going to be no Tesco's boy. I nodded my head to that. We got to his estate, an estate where worms come out at night. The meter was showing twelve, but I'm going to give it to him for ten. I'll do that if I'm heading home, do it for my yin and yang.

Fuck it, I liked him. "Have it for ten," I said.

He leant in my window and said "See you cock."

Bang and he's off. His legs going up and down, ankles moving his white socks along. He even had a limp, and he's across the road, smashing through a door. I watched, didn't move from my seat, what's the point? He'd sucked me in, ran away. He told me his stories, setting me up, for his get away. I was left with twelve on the meter, not a penny in my hand. He'd done a runner. He'd turned into a runt. I flicked my switch, turned the meter to zero, went home. Home's no better. Home's where the heart is, that's what they say. My heart isn't at home anymore.

Put a man and a woman in a room, overnight, and a baby will come out. That's what Nan would say. I thought it was madness. Not now.

I don't know who I am, and what I'm capable of. I've never known what I wanted to be.

Who does? Idi Amin, he knew. He gave himself the Victoria Cross for being so brave. Michael Jackson's got one as well. And I know for sure, Prince Charles's got a chest full of medals. For what?

The first thing I failed was my eleven plus. I couldn't go to my brother's school. I had a D instead of a C. I was eleven, and shit out of luck. He took the bus one way, me the other.

I've got to stop thinking. What's a man if he doesn't think? No better than a rabbit. I should leave myself alone. Shouldn't pick on myself. But I do.

I've just walked past a row of forget-me-nots and a dead rabbit. I'm with my girl, Lucy. She saw the rabbit too. Its eyes had already been had, by the things that want dead rabbit's eyes. Flies had taken the eyeball's place, all buzzing around trying to get their little bit of space in the socket. I look away and think about Nan again. I'm not a Nanna's boy, they don't exist.

Nan was given royal toilet paper once. It had the Queen's head on it, the faster you pulled the quicker went the head. I went round one afternoon. Nan grabbed me and said,

"Don't tell your Mum but have a look who's in the loo."

I thought she'd hidden someone, maybe an uncle or an aunt. I ran in, looked behind the door, in the bath, I couldn't see anyone.

"There's no one here," I shouted down the stairs.

"In the toilet, look in the bloody toilet," she shouted back.

I lifted the seat, I didn't know who I'd find. Then I saw the Queen sitting there. Nan hadn't even flushed after she'd been. I knew it was the Queen, I'd seen her on the box.

That's what we called TV. The box. When we got our first box, Dad carried it like a new-born child. We stood there, waited as he plugged the thing in. Nan came round and said to Dad,

"What, ain't there any cowboys on? These things are made for the cowboy and his gun." We weren't watching anything with cowboys in.

It wasn't long before Glad got her own TV. She got it from Kissing Frankie Knight. He got his name because he kissed like Gary Cooper. "What's a man if he can't kiss?" Glad would say. He was a lodger who helped with the rent. I remember bouncing on his knee and something growing in his pants. I didn't know what it was then. It was just the friction, he never did anything wrong. Kissing Frankie drove a truck and drank, that's what he did. Glad found him in a cupboard at the Hospital, sleeping like a dog. He stayed with them until he had a stroke.

A policeman and a thief under one roof. Grandad was a park policeman, walked round and round a park. This one Friday Glad came home with a TV on her back. The story goes, that when Bert came in for his tea, he saw it sitting there in the corner and said,

"Where the hell did you get that?"

"Frankie Knight. One kiss got me that."

Frankie had a soft spot for Nan. Bert didn't mind, he got a grapefruit every morning and an apple for lunch. One kiss got her first TV. My Dad paid for his, kept the receipt stuck on top.

Forget-me-nots brush against my feet and Lucy squeezes my hand.

I'm glad to be out of my cab, my rolling box, the hand thumping traffic. Me going mad. People with road rage and madness in their eyes. I beeped at one the other night. One small beep of the horn. I didn't mean anything by it, just warning him, letting him know I was there. He took it the wrong way. People do. He pulled up at the lights. And said. "Youuu dooo thatt again, I'll keeel you." He had an accent but I'm not supposed to notice that. It was Eastern European, let's say Kosovan.

"What? What, this?" I hooted the fucking horn. I kept my hand on the thing. Beeping away, I held it there, and grinned. I'd gone cuckoo.

"Yoouu fuckking dooo that one more…." he said.

I did, and again. Madness. He had these eyes, so I said to him.

"You got any kids?" I was smiling as I said it.

"Me? I have a son."

"Yeah." I nodded my head and said "And I bet you he's as thick as you." I didn't know I was going to say that, it just came out.

The man's door was already open but the lights had gone green. It wouldn't have been a good time to talk anymore. So I left him. Him with his madness, me with mine.

Chapter 2

One doesn't expect to lose his wife, his brother on the same day. That ain't normal that ain't right. I think I have. I loved them both.

"Some people bury their cats, don't they?" Lucy says, taking my hand. I look down at her, look into her eyes. All I see is eyes. The madness of eyes. Staring out my window, looking at eyes, eyes looking at me.

"Yeah, I guess some people do," I say, but I haven't thought about what Lucy just said.

We're sitting on a rock. We drove here, came up on the motorway, me up front, Lucy in the back. The cab smoking, rattling away on the motorway, overtaken by everything. I run my fingers over Lucy's. We're overlooking a village, it took hours to get here. I wanted it to take hours, could have taken a week. We were lucky we got caught in a pile up, the tail end. We had to wait while the blue lights came and picked up the mess. There was flesh, someone wasn't making it home for tea.

"Do some people bury their cats?"

"Yeah, some people bury their cats. Ancient Egyptians used to shave off their eyebrows when they lost their cats, they loved their cats," I smile. They did, never kill a cat in Egyptian times, you'd be taken outside and a spear would be driven through your heart. Those Egyptians, they loved a cat. They mummified thousands of them, some got sent to Liverpool where they were turned into manure. Lucy likes a question.

"Why we here Dad?"

"That's a good question, Lucy, that's a good question. I don't know." I haven't a clue.

There's a pause. Silence. Ten pence sheep walk around in the distance. That's what they're worth, I heard it on the radio driving up here. Lucy looked out the window in the back. I listened about sheep.

"If I die, will you bury me?" And after she's said it she looks at me.

It must be the rabbits, they're all over the hill limping, dying, or dead. Myxomatosis, we talked about it coming up the hill. I had to talk about it, the hill was crawling with them, the smell was rotten and the flies were waiting.

I've got sickness in my stomach. I've been carrying it with me. It lies in my stomach like a serpent's tail.

"I won't bury you darling, you'll live longer than me, that's the way these things work. You can bury me, or burn me, I don't care which. Do what you like with me."

Lucy looks at me, then pushes her face into my coat, cries. I pull her close, stroke her hair, feel her trembling body. Why did I say that? I'm not being a good Dad today, some days you fail. Just don't fail too often.

"What, darling? What?"

"I don't want you to die. I don't want you to ever die. I don't want you to leave me."

"I won't die darling, I won't die." And it's a lie. We all fucking die, the wise men and the fools.

"I don't want you to ever die."

"I won't darling. I promise. I'm going to live forever, longer," I say.

She squeezes my hand, we're silent. The wind blows the long grass, it dances around our feet, and the hills show us their colour. They could be doing a lot more than that, but I'm not very good at geography, you lose it in London.

"Why are we here Dad?"

She breaks the silence. Breaks my thought.

"I wanted to get away from London."

"Are we away from it here?"

"No, I guess not."

I smile. It's a sad smile. I hope she doesn't see it. I can't hide my sadness, it starts at my toes and comes all the way to my head. Makes a funny sound in my throat.

"Why? Why aren't we away from London?"

"Some things you just can't get away from."

"I'm hungry Dad, I want something to eat."

Oh god. "Come on darling, it's getting cold anyway, let's go get something to eat."

We get up, walk down the brown, dying hill. "Why are there so many blind rabbits Dad?"

"Well, it's a disease they get that makes them go blind, I told you, Myxomatosis, it does something to their eyes so they can't see."

"Do we go blind like that, so we can't see?"

I look at her.

"Sometimes we go blind, so we can't see." Oh, I go blind.

"Then what do we do?"

"We get a dog, a blind dog, sorry a guide dog and they help us."

She stops on the hill, bends down over a dead brown rabbit. Looks at it. I stop and stare down at it.

"If I went blind, would I remember what you looked like?" Lucy says, still looking at the rabbit.

"Well, what are you, six? I reckon you would, you wouldn't forget."

"If I close my eyes, I know what you look like. I can see you."

And she has her eyes closed, looking up at me. She's not cheating, they're closed.

"And if I close my eyes, I can see you darling."

I do, I close my eyes, and for a moment I see in darkness.

"Can blind people see things with their eyes shut?"

I open my eyes. See my darling's face. "I don't know"

"Can they see anything or is it just dark?"

"I really don't know."

She closes her eyes and I follow her in again.

"Can you see me, Dad? Can you see me with your eyes shut?"

"Yes, I can see you." I haven't stopped looking, since she was born. I even stare when she's asleep. Stand quietly, watch her cuddling her bear in her dreams. The bear's getting old, losing its stuffing, being cuddled to death.

"I can see you, it's good isn't it? I know exactly what you look like."

I open my eyes, she's smiling, holding her eyes shut with her fingers.

"And what can you hear?" I ask

"I hear, I hear your breath," Lucy says.

I listen to it. Its loud unrest. Can she hear the unrest? I don't want her to hear that, that can come later in her life.

Her unrest can come from her, not me.

"Come on darling, let's go. Let's get something to eat."

We make our way down, holding hands, over rabbits. The living, the limping, the dead. I've got to think of something to say.

"Did you know that rabbits are lucky? They have lucky feet. Grandad used to have one in his pocket all the time," I say.

He did, he's just died, another one for the sky. I was thinking about him as I walked over the rabbits. He had a foot in his pocket and a picture of an Indian on his arm. Dodge the Bodge, Bertie, Bert, a man of many names. A child miner, tinner, a bricklayer, and a park policeman to boot.

Sick in Sidcup, sick up Kent. Hops and barley, chow and fowl. Nan had been carting in more and more fruit to compost by his dying side. He loved his grapefruits, cut in half, eaten under washing hung above his head. My Mum, Pat to Grandad, Rita to Nan, they never could make up their minds, so they decided on, you call her that and I'll call her this, had been ringing me, telling me to go and see him, that it might be my last chance.

So I got in my cab, it was a Friday, the last day of the week. To go and see the man who'd carved my name in a tree. He took me in front of an old propped up tree and said, "this tree will be here longer than you and me." I noticed a heart, carved into the bark.

"I cut that heart. I did that for your Nan." In the heart it said, love never dies.

"Don't say a word, keep watch." And he started carving into the tree. He'd stop every now and then, make sure he wasn't being watched. Slowly a picture of an Indian came out on the tree, the same one he had on his arm.

He didn't get it done in one day, we came back to finish it off.

When it was done, he carved 'Nick' and said "Don't say a word, this is your's and my place now."

He'd tell stories about that Indian. I'd believe every word. He thought they were the only free men. "Some people hold onto shit like it's money, believe they own rivers. How can a man own running water? Water that goes on and on."

He'd talk like that, I think that's why the other policemen thought he was odd. He'd stopped having lunch with them years before. He ate on his own. I don't think they even liked talking to him.

I drove with sadness in my heart for company. I parked the cab, climbed the echoing, wood handled stairs. With nurses squeaking by, ticking swinging clocks, patients in pyjamas struggling along. Some would make it through the night, others would be dead. Hospital's not the best place to be.

At the ward I peered through the small square glass. By Bert's bed was Glad on death-watch, in her red-riding hood coat, she was sitting there, trying to save him from the wolf. Staring at the bed covers, tutting, shaking her old head into the air. The ward was full of the old, the cloth, the skin.

Grandad was on a ward of men with one way tickets. Men with tubes into arms, carrying blood from bags, and cards resting by drinks, "wishing luck." They needed more than luck here.

I walked over to Nan and kissed her. Then I turned, looked at Grandad. He had shrunk, a man child, his eyes a milky blue. His white hair sticking up in a petrified state. Grandad needed long johns to sleep in. You had to be careful with his legs. I once caught a vein with my foot. He was tickling me under my arm, he stopped, he had tears in his eye. I carried on laughing, not realising what I'd done. Grandad got up, blood dripping down his leg. He didn't tell me off, didn't say a word, just walked into the bathroom and cleaned himself up. I followed the dripping blood.

"Nick's here," Nan yelled.

I moved closer, he grabbed my hand. He wouldn't let go, we didn't say a word. Stood there with me over the bed. I started to cry and said "Sorry". He tightened more and still he wouldn't let go. My tears dropped to his name tagged hand. I rubbed the tears into his oceaned skin, didn't say another thing. He knew and I knew that this was called looking at death.

A man from a bed shouted.

"Help, help me." He was asleep, I looked at him, he was in pain.

"He's always shouting that" Glad said, pointing to the man who cries for help.

"Who do you think he wants to help him?" I said.

"He ain't had one visitor. So whoever it is, they ain't listening, poor thing," Nan said, then turned away.

Then I left, I couldn't take it anymore, shared a lift going down with a woman, tears in her eyes, and tomorrow a long way off.

"Sorry, I'm very sorry" I said.

She huddled in the corner and cried. The doors opened, I left, turned, and the doors shut her inside.

I walked back to my cab, turned on my light and looked for living flesh. Some bum to put on my seat. The first fare was a mother, smoker, tight lined lip, with a daughter, diamond girl, dead ringer for our precious dead Diana, and we arrive and she said "terribly sorry, I only have a twenty, could you make it ten?" Oh I'll make it ten, I thought. She hadn't said a thing before that, her type wouldn't talk to an ape like me.

"Sure." I said "And don't your daughter look like dead Diana?"

I smiled, she didn't smile back.

"That's a very rude thing to say" she said. "Have you no respect?"

"No" I said.

"What's your number, I'm going to report you."

"You do that" I said. I didn't give a fuck.

As the Scots say, "I see you."

I see the peacocks as they come out of shops, see cocks walking blocks, poodles and losers, and the winners, who take all. I see you. I see you in my mirror, on my seat. I see you. I hear you.

What a mess.

Chapter 3

The next morning I got a phone call from Nan.

"He's gone, he's buggered off, gone and left me this time."

I knew who'd gone, but I still said,

"Who? Who's gone?"

"Bert" she said. "Bert's gone. He's gone and done it, he's left me this time."

Then she put the phone down.

She loved her Bert, even broke into the church to marry him. It was closed, it was after midnight. They didn't do midnight marriage services then, so they went in through a window, him in his best clothes, her in hers. Said their vows to an empty church. Just the two to them, both saying "I do."

Bert took out a ring, put it on her finger. They didn't need a certificate, they didn't need a song, they had each other. Kissed and left by the window through which they'd come.

That was a long time ago.

I went with her to choose his box. It was the cheapest in the catalogue, a box made of wood. It wasn't cherry or walnut, they came on page twenty two, where the prices got high. A woman with folded arms watched from a high back chair. She looked more upset than Nan, sombre, with a cross around her neck, it shone as I looked at it.

"Oh that's a nice one" she'd say as our fingers turned a page.

"Oh yes, now that one I can really recommend."

Every time she said something, I'd look at her, then back at the page. I was looking at coffins but thinking about my brother, Gary, and Pam. When we got to page eighteen Nan looked at the woman and said

"We'll have the cheapest one you've got."

She'd finished with the book.

She held out her hand and I got up and pulled her up out of the seat. Deal done. A hole waiting for Grandad and his box.

I thought the woman had finished, she hadn't.

"With or without handles? Brass or wood?"

She said from her straight back chair, with her Sunday smile. A Christian. She'd make Sunday a non-swearing day. Clean, all the way to her pants. She stood up in her shoes, with the book in her hand, the cross shining around her neck.

"The cheapest" Nan said, her back already parting, from the drawn purple curtained room. She didn't look at the woman with the cross, she'd seen enough of coffins and their bits.

"Without handles then" the woman said, smiled, and I smiled back. Nan already had a stocking through the door, woe in her chest. I followed behind. Then the woman said,

"Would you mind closing the door?"

I'd forgotten.

"Sure" I said, turning.

Nan was by my side, she elbowed me and said,

"Don't you bother." So out of respect, just like that Dead Diana's mother said, I didn't. The door was left open wide.

You listened to my Nan.

She used to watch me play football, she'd stand there in her camel coat, with rings on her fingers, stockinged legs open wide. You could smell her from the pitch, she stunk, still does. Shouting at anyone who came close. In the end she was asked to leave. I was near by when the manager ran over and said, "Would you please not swear, love, not in front of the kids."

"Swear? I've hardly fucking started" she said, standing there in her camel coat, legs open wide. "No wonder these boys have no balls. Look how they fucking tackle." She held her own crutch as she spoke to the coach, and squeezed her camel coat. Nan liked a leg thumping tackle. She'd check my bruises when I came off the pitch.

I was dropped shortly after. Nan said she'd go down and have a word. I said, "No, please don't."

So her and her camel coat stayed indoors. We were never too young to be sworn at, she was the first woman ever to say the word fuck. I heard it one holiday.

We'd be packed off for two weeks, taken down to a lard infested tent. She's lived, washed and cooked in lard, it drips from the ceiling to the plates. But her heart keeps ticking. It has never been told it's bad. It gives her no pain, just waits for its next shot of lard.

We'd be perched on some hill, by a tree, near the sea. As long as Nan could see the sea, smell the chips, she was fine. It's put me off vinegar ever since.

We'd run around earning stripes for our cowboy hats. Grandad drew them on in marker pen, you saluted him when it was done. I got to sergeant in one week. Gary only made one stripe. He'd hidden Nanna's whisky, he wouldn't tell her where it was. Then she yelled, "Look, where is it? I can't fucking sleep without it. You want me not sleeping? Go and get me my fucking drink."

Gary went and got her whisky. He knew she would have hunted him down, other kids weren't allowed in our tent, what with the swearing coming out. You'd hear parents saying,

"Don't go near those boys' tent," as we walked past.

Grandad loved cowboy films. The last one I saw with him was at Greenwich. I took him to the pictures, a Clint Eastwood film. Halfway through Grandad was still holding his popcorn cup. Every time he took some, he knocked my arm, rattled the cup. And every time he did it, I said. "No thanks."

It was a big sized American cup. When we came out,
he said,

"Clint's getting old, I was watching him, he's not as quick going for his gun." I hadn't noticed. Grandad smiled, we walked on. That was the last cowboy film I watched with him, the one where Clint was slow with his gun, and he offered me his popcorn cup.

Chapter 4

Lucy jumps another rabbit. This place is full of rabbits, or are they hares?

"Can I have one? Can I have a lucky rabbit's foot?"

I look at it, with its eyes, its tongue hanging out.

"Not one of these, these aren't lucky, these aren't lucky rabbits."

They don't look lucky from where I'm standing, they look like shit. No one cared for these rabbits.

"Which are the lucky rabbits Dad?"

And she's got one eye shut, and the other looking at me. My Lucy waiting for an answer. An answer I can't give.

"I don't know, I'll get you one from a shop. They only sell lucky ones in shops."

"When?"

"When we find a shop. Anyway we have to eat first, remember you said you were hungry."

"I want to be lucky, is it good to be lucky?"

"It helps darling, it really helps. It's better to be lucky than not."

"Are you lucky Dad. Are we lucky?"

Ha, I look away, stare into the distance, I used to think I was luck. Lucky bastard, I used to think. But that changes with age, time and all the shit that gets dumped in the mind, taken to your spirit, polluting, seeping into you.

"I'm lucky to have you, I'm definitely lucky to have you."

And I am. I'm glad I said it.

"And Mummy, and Uncle Gary" Lucy says.

"Ha."

That's all I can say to that.

Lucy has her back to me, I'm glad. I don't want her to see me. Not now, I've got tears in my eyes. And this year's loving is over.

My stomach kicks. Knotted. Sick. It's all to do with what's running in my mind. If your mind won't leave you alone, it means you haven't a friend up top. No one's looking after you.

Drops of rain start to fall.

"I love you so much, don't you forget that, Lucy. You mustn't ever forget that. Never forget that your Dad loves you."

"I love you Daddy, I love you lots and lots. You can love more than one person can't you Daddy?"

"Yes. Yes you can darling."

"Because I love you, I love Mummy, I love Uncle Gary, Granny."

Then she stops, goes silent, she's trying to think of someone else she might love.

"I know you do, I know you do."

She turns, raises her arms. She looks no different to when she was two.

"Carry me Dad?"

"Sure darling." I bend down scoop her up, squeeze her leg. She's getting big now. Where did the time go?

"Can we run down the hill? I know, you be the horse."

And that's what I want to do, run, I want to run, run down this hill, down another and far, far away. Keep running till I reach the sea, have a seagull pick me up and set me free. I loved that Jonathan Seagull, he was a good flier.

"Let's go, yea ha!" I force it out, the little cowboy in me, the cowboy put in by Glad and Bert. But it's got no yip in it. No loud yea ha!

Lucy's laughing, shouting "Go faster, faster." She's happy. She bounces on my shoulders, her laughter makes her light. We make our way over the rabbits and down the hill. I see my black cab. It's vacant light not on. It looks lonely, out of place. Sitting on wood chip, with no fare in sight.

My stomach's sick. I'm thinking again. It's all I've been doing. Thinking about the two of them going at it. One rabbit on top, my brother, my wife. Bastards. I'm seeing it in detail, bums going up and down. It's my own horror porno movie, starring my brother and my wife. I've spent too much time driving at night, living in my head.

When I put the key in the cab I knew I wouldn't make it that day. I didn't have it in me, what with Grandad being dead. I did a little scratching here and there, but I gave up, my heart wasn't in it. I came home. I found a gap in the traffic, that street that no one knew. People still believe they exist, that quiet unknown street, with you and a clear road in sight. They don't. I fucking tell them, those roads don't exist. They don't, but passengers still want me to look. Looking for some lost treasure.

I opened the door to the flat, we're up with the pigeons, the clouds, the snot, the rain, the shit. And noise travels up. I tell Lucy we're nearer to God.

As I came in, Pam came out of the bathroom, a towel round her waist, her hair down. She looked great, beautiful. She's getting better as she ages. She's all I've ever wanted in a woman. Nothing more. She's my mate, the best one I've ever had, the only one I've got.

"Oh, hello love, didn't hear you come in." I'm sure she said it loud. But that's now. That's now I think that. I didn't then. It was just a sad day coming home to see my wife.

"I couldn't be bothered with it, love. You look great" I said. I'm sure I said that.

I kissed her, touched her, ran my fingers down her body, down the towel. I looked at her. Moved my hand under the towel, stroked her leg, used my fingers. Took the towel from her body, let it drop to the floor. Ran my fingers through her fingers, ran them up her arm to her mouth, drew the outline of her lips. Kissed her.

"Not here, love, not here, let's go in our room."

"Gary's not in?"

"No, he's out, gone for a swim."

Gary doesn't swim. But I didn't think that as she took my hand, walked me to the bed. I had other things on my mind. Lucy was at a friend's house. We had time.

"Gary might come back" Pam said, closing the door.

"You look great Pam, you look great." I kissed her. I love her. It's got better over the years. Her and Lucy, they're what I've got, that's me, that's what keeps the wheels turning. They're my life.

We lay next to each other, Pam's head on my chest, me stroking her hair.

"I've got something to tell you" Pam said. Then I heard the door go.

"Hello, anyone in?"

"Yeah, we're in here" Pam said, looking at me.

"Nick back?" Gary says.

"Yeah, I'm in here, I came back home early, I couldn't take any more shit."

He knocked on the door, came in, his hair wet.

"How you feeling?"

Pam's known him for years, since we were all kids. Pam was Gary's first girlfriend. I remember seeing them kissing on a sofa, me and the party going on around. That never stopped them going at it.

"Sad, but I'm alright, and you?"

"I'm all right, been for a swim."

"Didn't know you swam?"

"I'm going to get fit, I'm fed up with being unfit."

"Yeah, I should do that."

Gary smokes and drinks too much.

He left the room. Pam lifted her head off my chest. I kissed her again and then she left the room. Followed Gary out.

I took my naked body to the bathroom. The floor was wet, Pam's pants on the floor. I picked them up, smelled them, and put them on top of the toilet. The shower curtain was pulled.

Lucy asks,

"What we going to eat, Dad?"

I've got to be a better Dad, stop thinking about what's running inside of me. Give Lucy a happy day out. It's not every day you get to be free of London, see a hill, breathe some air.

"I thought we'd go into the village, there must be something there. Get some chips or something."

We walk the rest of the way to the cab in silence.

I fire the cab up and drive to a village, it's quiet, and it's got a long name. When you leave London it's all quiet. There's a pie shop open with its red neon sign. We go in, a bell goes above our head. I look up, then at the big woman who wants to serve.

"Hiya, how are you two?" she says, smiling, her pies in a cabinet and her chips frying.

"We're fine" I say, raise my cheeks, push out that smile. Smile to people you don't know.

"Daddy's going to get me a lucky rabbit foot" Lucy says. She likes to talk to people. She talks and I hold her hand.

"Is that right?" The aproned one smiles at Lucy, then at me.

"Yes, rabbits are lucky, did you know that?" Lucy says.

"Yes I did, young lady."

"Daddy told me, his Grandad kept one in his pocket. Didn't he, Dad?"

I nod my head, give the lady another smile.

The woman leans over and strokes Lucy's hair, gives me another smile.

"Thanks. Thanks a lot." I hand her the money and leave. Leave with our chips and our pie. When we're out of the shop Lucy says,

"I like it here Dad, do you? She was a nice lady, wasn't she?"

"Yes, darling."

But I'm a London pigeon, my wings are clipped, I'm stuck with my mind inside the M25. It's where I hunt for money, it's all I know.

I can't eat. My mind won't leave me alone. I've got to make a friend of my mind.

I walk over to the bin and put our papers in. I tap on the window and the woman smiles, I mouth "Watch this." She looks at me. I get back in the cab and do a three sixty and another and another. Going round and around in the road outside her shop.

Lucy's laughing, the woman stares. I do about five or six then stop. I feel dizzy.

"Hey Gary, you got a razor? Mine's as blunt as fuck."

I shouted from the bathroom, he was in the living room with Pam.

"Yeah, sure, in my toilet bag. On the shelf."

Gary's two years older. We're sort of close, then other times not, but he's the only brother I've got. He's left his wife, they'd stopped kissing, they couldn't even look at each other. He'd counted every day they hadn't kissed. He left on day four hundred and sixty-six.

When Gary came to leave he said, 'I'm leaving now, I'm on day four hundred and sixty-six.'

"Oh," his wife said. "Goodbye."

"I mean it, I'm really leaving now, I'm on four hundred and sixty- six kissless days and that seems as good as any time to leave."

"Ok." That's all she said back to him. That's Gary's story anyway. I believe him. One never knows what goes on behind closed doors. She wasn't one for words. She read like a chain smoker, read one after the other. Didn't look up from her book. Not even when me and Pam went round, you talked to her in between her pages. She might have been bright, she might have been dull, I never knew. She was always quiet. They never popped out a kid and she didn't like it when we played cards.

Our Dad, he liked poker, he liked it a lot. He had poker eyes, eyes you couldn't read. He liked Americans because they invented poker.

Me, I'm not sure. I had this couple in, check shirts, Texan tans. We're driving along when he says from the back of the cab, "Right, stop the cab, stop it here. I know what you're doing, stop it here." He's about seventy five and he's having a go. So I pulled it over. "I know what you're doing, going round and around. Call a Bobby, Meryl, call a Bobby." And he sat there and waited for a Bobby to appear.

Dad was a poker man with poker eyes. A ten pound a pot man. That's as high as he'd go. Once a week he'd go to his club, his table, and turned his cards, tried his luck. When I was young he'd take us to watch him play, the only kids in the club.

"Never show weakness, always make your eyes lie"
he'd say.

"How do you make your eyes lie?" Gary used to ask.

"You'll figure that out when you get older."

And he has, he's managed to do that quite nicely. Fucking thinks I don't know what they're doing.

We'd all go round to Dad's on a Sunday, once a month and

37

play our cards. Even when I got married we'd still go round. But Gary's wife, she was different. She didn't come back after the first time. Dad asked her to play poker, he'd ask anyone, "Play poker with us Claire?"

"Sure" she said.

"I'll play you for your clothes" he said.

"You're joking?" Then Claire looked at Gary, and Gary looked at Dad. Pam and I laughed. Pam had played, Dad had seen her breasts, so had Gary, maybe that's when it started.

"No, that's how we play" Dad said.

Gary should have told her, it's what we did, play for our clothes. We'd turn the heating down in winter, up in summer. Sweat or freeze. It upped the stakes. That was all part of it. Dad played it in his Navy days.

"You learn more from a person with no clothes on than you do from a lifetime's chat," he'd say.

He had tattoos, on his front, on his back. He was covered in them. A big ship, with his shipmates on his front, Jesus and the disciples on his back. I asked him about Jesus once, he said, "He's a good man to have watching your back."

So Claire said, "Gary take me home now."

"One hand?" Dad said, still wanting to play.

"I want to go, I want to go now," she said, standing. She never went back. That sort of thing doesn't happen in her family.

When Gary got married, Dad was sitting next to me. Claire didn't want him there, on account of the poker thing. He pulled on my jacket sleeve and whispered, "What's he gone and done, son?"

"I've no idea, Dad" I said back. I didn't.

Later, at the reception, he got them all playing poker and fleeced the lot.

I unzipped Gary's brown toilet bag, four razors and some cream, one durex, wrapped in silver, blue writing down it. He must have got it in Europe, I couldn't understand the writing. I looked back at the durex, lying in a bag, waiting to be put on. I put the bag back. I had a shave, felt good. I put a towel around my waist, went into the front room. Pam and Gary were talking.

Pam turned. "Very handsome" she said as I walked in. Gary didn't turn his head from the TV.

He's been with us for two long weeks.

"Will I miss school again tomorrow?" Lucy says from the back of the cab. It's a big space back there. She can't hit the floor with her feet. Nor do her seat belt up, I get in the back, clip her in.

"Thanks, Daddy. Will I miss school?" She asks again. Already on the make for another day off. Who can blame her, life's choke put on you at such a young age.

"I think so, is that alright?"

She nods her head, it's more than alright for her. If I knew what I was going to do next I'd do it, but I don't, so we sit and wait.

After work the next day I had a shower.

Gary's toilet bag still on the shelf, open. I looked at the bag, washed under my armpits, looked at the bag. And there was something, something. I picked it up, moved the razors to one side. The silver durex was gone. I looked through the razors, gone. I looked again, still gone.

I was in the shower, the toilet bag filling with water. Water running onto razors.

I zipped the bag up, felt a pain in my chest. I got out and sat on the toilet, the toilet bag at my feet. Sitting there with water running off my back, hitting the floor. I sat there, sat there, for I don't know how long.

"What do you want for dinner love?" Pam shouted from the kitchen. I didn't answer, my mouth was dry and I was shaking. I remember all this so slowly, clearly.

"Pam wants to know what you fancy for dinner?" Gary said, outside the door.

"I heard what she fucking said." I paused, then I said "Did you go out today, Gary?"

I was sitting on the toilet, with my head in my hands.

"No, didn't do a thing. You know what I'm like."

"No I don't know what you're like. So you didn't go out?"

"No."

I kicked the toilet bag against the door. Got up, put the towel around my waist and opened the door. Went into our bedroom. Pam's pants were on the floor, I bent down and picked them up, spun them round and put the crutch to my nose.

Lucy's looking at me, I try to smile.

"Daddy," she says "Dad, who made the first dog?"

How the hell do I know? But I've got to answer, that's what a Dad's for. I've got to stay calm, in control. Got to.

"I don't know, love, I haven't got a clue." I'm trying to remain calm for Lucy, trying to hang on, be that good Dad.

"Did it belong to Adam and Eve?"

"Yeah, I think you're right, it belonged to Adam and Eve." I laugh. "The first dog belonged to those two."

"Not everyone believes in Adam and Eve, do they?"

"Not everyone, no."

"Do you, Dad?"

"Well, that's a hard one."

"Why?"

Lucy sits and waits, she'll always wait for an answer.

"Sometimes, but not always, sometimes it's hard to."

"Why Dad, why is it sometimes hard to?"

"Well, sometimes things don't seem to be very just, not right."

"What does just mean?"

"Fair, sometimes things aren't fair."

"Sometimes my friends don't want to play with me, that's not fair is it?"

"No, that's not fair" I say. "I'll always play with you, though."

"I know you will Daddy. I don't like it when people won't

play with me at school."

She sits back in her seat, looks out the window, I turn from her and look out of mine. And we wait, we're waiting for me.

A tear runs down my cheek, another, another. I can't help myself. I keep looking out the window, I can't stop. 'Stop.' I say, gritting my teeth. But I can't, and so they come.

Lucy looks at me.

"Dad," she says, "Daddy, you're crying."

"I know darling, I know. Tonight we might end up sleeping in the car. Is that OK, is that alright? It's just that I've got nothing planned."

It's getting dark, so I drive into a field, turn the cab lights off, darkness. I pick up the sleeping bags and get in the back with Lucy. She's tired, confused. I left a note for Pam on the table this morning, saying I was taking her out of school for the day. We do that sometimes, take her to the zoo, a museum. I got in the cab this morning, and drove her away. Left Pam with Gary and the note. She'll be worried, I should give her a ring. I feel the phone in my pocket but I'm not going to call her, not now. Why the fuck should I? Do they realize what they've done?

Chapter 5

Lucy puts her head in my lap.

"Tell me a story about Grandad?" She thinks I've been crying over Grandad, she's trying to be nice.

I close my eyes.

"Lucy you know what? You're a lovely girl." She is, always has been. "Well, Grandad used to find orphaned dogs, lots of them, and bring them home. Big Nanna would open the door and say "Not another silly beep dog."

Lucy knows all about Glad's swearing and her potato humping hips.

Lucy looks up.

"Why does big Nanna swear so much? She does, doesn't she?"

I look down, stroke Lucy's head.

"She sure does, some people do. She always has, that's why your Granny can't stand swearing."

"She's a bit posh, isn't she, Granny? She doesn't like it when you or Uncle Gary swear, does she? She tells you off."

Mum can't stand swearing, she says it makes her feel sick. If you want to talk to her, just don't swear or she'll stop listening.

"What happened to the dog?" Lucy says, she never forgets where she is, where she's up to in a conversation.

"So Grandad says yeah, another dog's been left. And big Nanna went and got some milk."

"See, that's nice. Even though big Nanna swears, she's nice, she didn't have to get some milk but she did, didn't she?"

"Yes she did, sometimes people growl more than they bite."

"Dogs growl, don't they? There's one in the park that growls, but if you say good boy, good boy, it stops. I used to be scared of it, I'm not now."

She looks up, smiles. She doesn't look so tired now.

"That's good, it's good not to be scared of things."

I'm looking at her, but I'm thinking of them, Pam and Gary.

"Then what?" Lucy says.

I look at her, she likes a story, that's how she learnt to talk.

"So Grandad says to Nanna. "These people come to the park with dogs, leave with leads. How can they forget they came with a dog?"

Lucy's excited, she wants to say something.

"That's stupid, imagine forgetting you've got a dog." And she laughs, and waits for me to laugh. So I laugh.

"Grandad had this dog once, it could balance on a ball. It used to play outside, practise. You'd look out the window and it would be balancing on a ball. You didn't even have to tell it to do it. It just liked doing tricks."

"Really, it just liked doing tricks. So it would just do it, you didn't have to tell it to. Was this the dog Nanna gave milk too? What was its name?"

A hundred and one questions from my darling one.

"I think they called it Sam. Grandad used to say who could forget a dog like that?"

"Some people are silly, aren't they Dad?"

And I say it very slowly. "Some people are very silly."

I've still got the pain in my gut to prove it. Thoughts in my head to live with. Pam, Gary, Glad and Bert and a job I can't

45

take.

"Did they keep it?"

I look at her, what's she talking about? I've completely forgotten what we were talking about. I'm doing that more and more.

"Did they keep the dog, Daddy?"

And now I remember. "Yeah, yeah they kept it until it died."

Lucy shakes her head, maybe I shouldn't have said that.

"Grandad and big Nanna must have been sad, I would have been sad, if I'd had a dog like that. I'd never want it to die."

"They were upset, and now young lady close your eyes and go to sleep."

"One more story, Dad, just one more, tell me about Grandad's pigeons, please?"

She looks at me.

She knows all about his pigeons it's a stalling tactic, she doesn't want to go to sleep.

Grandad was a park policeman for nearly thirty years. He'd cycle there on his bicycle, with his basket of birds up front. He'd let them out on the heath and they'd fly back home. I don't think the other two knew about Bert and his birds. They never even asked him about the basket. They were park police, you didn't have to be clever, just polite. Grandad was the first in the family to get a profession.

"Dad?" Lucy's looking up at me.

"Yes love?"

"Just one more story, please?" Her head's on my lap her hair over my leg. I can't refuse her.

"There was this once, I wasn't there but Nanna told me, that Grandad was so upset, that he put all his pigeons in a basket."

"Why was he upset, Daddy?"

"I'm going to tell you," I snap. Her lip goes. Why the fuck did I do that?

"I'm sorry love. I'm sorry." I stroke her hair until she smiles at me.

"Well he had this one bird, his favourite, Julius Caesar, it flew away and didn't come back."

Lucy sits up.

"Why Daddy, why didn't it come back?" She puts her finger to my face, wipes away a tear at my eye. Christ, I'm still crying and I didn't even know.

"Well Grandad didn't really know, so he took them all away on a train to where he was born, miles away, stayed away the night, like we are now."

"So he went miles and miles away."

I look out the window, it's a big dark night sky.

"Yes love. He didn't want any of his pigeons to come back. He thought it was something he'd done. He thought he hadn't cared for them, looked after them properly. That's why his Julius Caesar had gone. He'd never lost a bird before."

"So he was upset."

"It took them a couple of days, but every one of those birds came back. So then he knew it was nothing he'd done, it wasn't him."

"So they all came back? What even Julius Caesar?"

"No I don't think he came back, now night night."

"Are you sad Daddy?"

"No I'm fine, now goodnight."

"Night, Daddy."

"Night, love."

I lean forward and kiss her on her lips, wait for her dreams to carry her away. And it's quiet now. No one's here, just me and Lucy in a field.

I sit in darkness with her head on my lap, her breathing taking her away to her dreams. Me sitting with my thirty eight year old unrest. I've spent fifteen years going round in circles, spinning on my wheels taking people to where they're going, and me? I've arrived at whatever place they call this.

I've got a Nan waiting in her flat, mourning, waiting for me to come round, to talk in my ear.

Chapter 6

"What bloody time did you get back? I can't wake Lucy, she's sound asleep. Wake up Nick." Pam's waiting for me to answer. I don't.

"She's got her SATs, you know that? I was worried out of my mind. Why was your phone turned off?" Pam says. Then says, "Worried sick I was." She's standing over me. I don't open my eyes. I don't want to see her, I can't.

"Late, it was late" I say with my eyes closed.

"Yeah, well thanks a lot. We've got to talk, I've got something to tell you."

"Tell me now" I say and open my eyes. "Go on, tell me Pam, tell me what you've got to say." I'm surprised at how loud I say it.

"Not now. I'm too angry with you." And she leaves the room, slamming the door.

Oh so reasonable, she is. "Oh, are you?" I shout at the door. I can hear her with Lucy. She's getting her up, getting her dressed, making her go to school. I lay in bed until the front door goes. I'm not up to seeing Pam. Gary's on the sofa, sleeping, snoring, happy. Contented bastard, sleeping the sleep of the sinner. I don't want breakfast with him. I pick up my taxi bag, put my badge round my neck.

"Is that you Nick?" Gary says from his back on the couch.

"Yeah, it's fucking me" I say and slam the front door.

I go down in the lift, walk through piss and puke to the cab. I'm not normally out this early. Up with school children on their merry way.

I heave my way into the traffic, get a morning bird. A tie round his neck, a briefcase on his lap, he sits there. I can see the yoghurt on his lips. I drop him and get another and another. Then a woman with a hat and she says,

"All my friends are so boring, I wish I could meet someone who was like me."

"What?" I'm in traffic, I don't know if I heard right. She repeats it. She says it again.

"Are you serious?" I say, waiting on a set of reds.

"Yes, you must know what I mean," she says.

"I've got no idea what the fuck you mean," I say. As the lights go green. She doesn't say anything. But I see her take out her pen, write down my number. There's another one going to try and make me lose my job.

"Well thank you." I say as she hands me a fistful of coins. "And did you write my number down correctly?"

"Yes I did," she says.

Fuck this, I'm not going to search for flesh today. Not going to drive around looking for a bum to put on the seat. I'll leave that for the others. They can divvy up my share, drive the bridges with lights for hire. Waiting to catch a finger, a command and a ride. Taking a him or a her to wherever they want to go. Today I'm not doing that. I give up. I've had enough. I'm not waiting for my yellow light to be taken into blue.

Blue, the colour of capture, someone sitting in the seat. I can drive with no hands. I've crossed the Thames many times on a midnight light. A ferryman dropping off his catch. Salmon out west. Cockles and mussels, north. Mackerels, east. Winkles and whelks, south. And minnows everywhere. I wouldn't know a pike if it bit me on the arse, but they're out there.

I fish on the currents of life. Now then, will I go left? Will I go right? Fuck it, I see a hairdresser's, and that's where I'm going. I get myself on to a rank, and shove my bag in the boot.

I walk in, it's empty, apart from a girl and her mirrors. She takes me to a seat, and throws the cape over my head, it flutters to a stop on my shoulder.

"Do whatever you like with me," I say.

"Sorry?" she says.

"Change me from whoever I am," I laugh. She gives me this look.

"So you want to look younger, is that right?" she says, with her blonde bob.

"I don't know what I want. I trust you," I say.

My hair gets shorter, turns from brown to blonde. And that's followed up for dessert with hoops through my tits. And when it's all done she says, "Well what do you think?"

"My tits are on fire," I say.

"Not your piercing, your hair?"

"Oh. It's OK."

"It's no worse than when you came in." And she smiles. I smile into the mirror, nod my head. Look down at my shirt and my throbbing tit.

"Thanks." I say and leave her with her potions, pins and guns, my nipples on fire. When I get out, I look back in at her, she's sweeping my hair away. A new me.

I walk two hundred metres down the road and see a pub. I go in, sit at the bar and take out my book. I look down at the page it says 'will the circle be unbroken.'

Something hits my shoe, I look down, it's a stick and it's white. I look up, a blind man. A man with no eyes. What he has got are red, red slits, nappy rash eyes. That's what comes into my mind as I see his eyes. Nappy rash eyes, things like that shouldn't happen but they do. Too much time on my own, in my cab, turning a wheel. So I stop looking and say,

"Sorry." It's the best I can do.

I said sorry, for him bumping into my foot. Saying sorry buys you time. Saying sorry in London is like air, as important as learning the map. And still some people don't use the word. I don't know.

"You don't know what?" the blind man says.

I look at him, I must have said it out loud. I've started thinking 'I don't know' about most things lately but I didn't realise I was saying it out loud. I thought I was keeping it in. Things are slipping out, since the durex thing.

"Sorry," I say back to him. "I was talking to myself."

He doesn't say anything, just rocks his head.

It's all that time up front of the cab, pulling people along, the ox up front, pulling people along. I take them to where they want to go and I'm left talking out loud.

"Any women here?"

The man with no eyes says, touches me with his stick, I guess he wants to make sure I'm still here, that I haven't gone.

"Women?" I say. I say it loud.

"Any women here? I'm blind, not deaf mate."

"Did I shout?"

"You sure fucking did." His head jerks after he's finished what he's got to say. Then it keeps on rocking, like his neck's on a spring. I'm staring at him, I haven't answered yet.

"Hello?" he says again. I think he thinks I've gone. His stick

53

hits my foot, that's the third time he's done that.

"Yeah, sorry, what did you say?" I say. Looking at his stick, resting against my accelerator foot.

"Women, are there any women in here?"

"Why, you meeting someone?"

I turn in the stool, looking for whoever it is he's looking for. But it's early and there aren't many people in, just earlybirds with nothing else to do.

"What does she look like, this woman?"

"I don't know. I haven't met her yet," he says.

What is this man talking about? If he wasn't blind, which he definitely is, this would be the time when I'd put my head in my book, wouldn't look back at him. I'd have him down as a nut, or one of those you get in the cab, who ask a question, with no time for an answer. The busy ones, the chosen alligator shoed ones.

I picked up this guy in the cab once, the first thing he says is,

"You don't like me do you?"

I'd just stopped, he was only just in, him and his silk socks. I hadn't made up my mind till he asked me that. Then I knew, I knew exactly what I felt about him and his socks.

But this man by my side is blind. You should be kind to the blind.

"What's that?" he says.

"What's what?" I say.

"You said something about silk socks."

"Did I?" I must be talking out loud again.

Then there's silence. If he had eyes he wouldn't like me staring at him, but I've got the eyes, he's got the slits. I lift up an ashtray, read what's on the back. If I hadn't given up smoking, I'd be putting one in. The ashtray's made in a place I've never heard of. So much to learn. Four months without a fag.

Pam says giving up put the dragon in me, on my tongue. I tell her it's the street. Some people are born with a silver spoon, others are born to choke. It's a back-breaking job, not in the swing axe way, you just slowly crush the spine. I'm a big man, shrinking, shrinking into the seat. Leaving skin, leaving a little of me.

The job won't keep you full but it will keep you fed. Hungry, the best way to be. Watch a shark circling, that be me. When I go home and sit in the darkness, after twelve hours behind the wheel, I do the two can pull. I take the can from the plastic trap, close the fridge door, walk to the chair, raise the can, drink. Do it all in silence, let Pam and Lucy do the sleeping. Well that's what I used to do, that was my thing. But now, who knows?

"So there's no women here?" he says, taking out a packet of cigarettes, putting one in his mouth. I look at him, he did that well. He lights it. Doesn't even burn his fingers, or burn his nose. I'm lucky he's got no eyes because I'm really staring. How will he know when he's coming to the end? I look at his fingers, they're not burnt, just brown, so he knows. "What does this woman look like? I'll see if I can see her," I say trying to help.

I haven't met many blind people. There was this blind boy waiting to watch a film once. I was young. The queue was long. I was waiting with Dad. I kept on staring at him, Dad bent down, whispered in my ear.

"Don't be rude."

He'd caught me.

"But Dad," I said back to him "Dad, how's he going to see the film?"

I didn't know. Dad was still bent by my ear.

"Don't worry, he'll figure out a way."

Dad must have liked that blind boy, he wouldn't always talk like that, wouldn't always whisper in my ear. Dad worked hard. He was tired all the time. He liked me to know just how hard he worked, how tired he was.

Then the blind man says something.

"Sorry?" I was in my head, I spend a long time in there. I haven't heard what he said.

"I don't know what this woman looks like, I haven't met her yet."

He's talking about this woman again. I've missed something.

"There are no women in here," I say turning in my stool, checking once more, one might have slipped in.

"I once met a girl here, nice girl, polite, friendly, if you know what I mean. It's been my lucky pub ever since. I don't normally go to pubs on my own. Things happen in pubs, they're full of smack heads, thieves and people who have nothing better to do than lift a glass and slobber. Mind if I sit down?" he says.

Now that's a speech. A real mind if I take my seat speech. He can't have me down as a smack head or a thief, maybe just someone who will slobber.

He starts to rock again.

When he talks he's still, and when he stops he rocks, I've noticed. He's got nappy rash eyes and a springy neck. He's pretty fucked really.

"Sure, here I'll get you a stool."

I stand up move around his back, pull him a stool. He's got jeans on, regular type, from behind you'd never know he was blind, just a bloke in his thirties standing in a pub, in jeans.

When I'm in front of him I say.

"Here."

Spinning the stool on one leg, till it comes to a stop. He puts his hand on top of mine, then slides it off, feels around the stool, climbs on, rests his stick by the bar.

"This is the Lord Clyde, right?" he says.

I don't know. I never know what pub I'm in. I know pubs I don't want to be in. I wouldn't want to be in a pub with Gary and Pam, not now, not how I'm feeling. I've got to sort things out.

I'm not much of a reader anymore, I don't even read menus, just hold it in my hands. I'll order the same as the person I'm eating with, or whatever stranger I'm next to. Or I'll say, "surprise me."

I go to this one cafe, they don't ask me anymore, I just sit there, they bring something out of the hatch. That's the way I like to eat, eating on the run. Then back in the saddle mounting up, ready to use my fishing eyes again.

The man with no eyes looks at me, I haven't given him the answer he needs.

"Is this the Lord Clyde?" he says again.

"I'll have a look, I'm not sure," I say, getting off my stool. He beats me to it.

The blind man shouts at the bar. The barman's behind, cleaning glasses, a magazine by his side, he's reading and wiping.

"Yeah?"

That's all he says, doesn't even look up. Just says yeah, with his Aussie accent. Doesn't take his eyes off the magazine. He's Australian, working his five pounds an hour, thinking of running with bulls, drinking in Munich and what sticker to put on his VW camper next. I see them out there. What's he want to look up for?

Thinking about the Aussie makes me think about a friend. One thing connecting to another, one bumper to the next.

He had a VW camper. He kept parking stickers on it, everywhere, he never took them off. All over it, front, side, every window. All he left was a little driving hole, to see out of. When he parked wardens had to look for his ticket, they had to be good at their job, keen. He'd always have one, you just had to look. Sometimes we'd sit in the van, watch a face looking for that ticket. He never told me why he did it. I didn't ask. I just liked the fact he did.

"Want a drink?" the blind man says, turning, bringing his red eyes to me. I stop thinking about my friend with his van.

"Sure, why not?"

Why not have a drink with a blind man? I'd only come in for one but what the hell, tomorrow's another sad day, what with putting Grandad in his box, wearing the black tie, then all this shit in my head.

"What you having?"

"Bitter, thanks, IPA, what's your IPA like mate?"

I look at the barman.

"I've never drunk the stuff mate. Wouldn't touch it," the barman says.

"That's handy to know. I'm a bitter man, even though it gives me the shits. Upsets my tummy, especially when the pipes in the pub aren't clean. Your pipes clean mate?"

Then I stop, the Aussie looks at me. Doesn't say a word, drops his eyes to read whatever he's reading. No answer.

Then the blind man says "Where you from?"

"Canberra."

But the Aussie doesn't go on, he's not going to talk. He's a barman who doesn't talk. Like a vicar in a pulpit, who won't give out any lines, won't show his flock the way.

The blind man rocks, then stops. And when he stops he's ready to talk again.

"I once went into a pub in Bristol, some place like that. Some strange land. I'd never been there before. We ordered our drinks and the landlord got a phone call. I listened, he talked. It was in his voice. He was serving us, talking on the phone at the same time. It was the voice, something in his voice. He was frightened, I could tell. Are you listening?" he says. The Australian's cool, just nods his head, carries on pouring the beer.

I turn, say to the blind man,

"Yeah, he's listening. He just nodded his head."

The barman looks straight at me. I point to the blind man's eyes.

He's not rocking, he's ready with his story.

"It was the way the landlord talked. Frightened to hell, scared out of his wits, he was. Anyway we took our drinks to our seats. When I was sitting I turned to my mate and said, what the fuck's up with that barman? My mate just said, what? Because he hadn't heard. So I told him, that bloke's shit scared of something.

We were staying in Bristol for like two or three days, and the next night it was on the news, landlord of pub found dead. I knew that man was frightened, and he knew he was frightened as well. You can't hide from your voice. They say a man can tell a lot by someone's eyes, I go by their voice." So, how much for the drinks?" he asks the man who won't talk.

"Three ninety."

The Aussie gives the blind man a look.

"Is that a true story?" I ask.

"Of course it is," he says, and the Australian looks at both of us.

It must be shit to sit in a pub if you're blind. It must be shit to be blind. I raise my glass, let the beer into my throat. To the blind man. The Aussie goes back to wiping, but not before he takes one last look.

The blind man goes into his pocket, pulls out a folded note.

"Here."

The bar man takes the note, doesn't say a word, unfolds the note, opens the till, puts the money in. Then centres the blind man's drink on the mat.

"Cheers." He turns to me.

"Cheers, I don't even know your name?"

In my head he's just the blind man, a blind man who rocks then stops then talks.

"Kenneth, but call me Kenny, I never liked the name Kenneth, it never sounded like me. My Dad liked Kenneth Williams. He liked what he did with his nostrils."

"What did he do with his nostrils?" I say.

"I never saw it," Kenny says back to me. "I'm blind."

"Of course you are," I say.

Kenny picks up his glass, holds it in the air, carefully I put my glass to his. "Cheers," we say at the same time.

"And yours?"

"Nick. Short for, my Dad couldn't think of a name."

If his eyes could see, he'd be looking at me.

"Nice to meet you Nick."

"Nice to meet you Kenny."

I smile at him, I don't know what else to say. So I don't say anything. Then I get up and say.

"I'll just go to the toilet."

I don't really want to go. I get off the stool, go into the toilet, stand looking at myself in the mirror. Fucking hell, what have I done. My hair, fuck. And my nipples. What have I done? I've aged, I'm so tired, my driving eyes sting. I'd rather have these than his. I close them tight, like Lucy did on the hill, try and walk to the door. I hit a sink. I can't even walk from here to the door. I open my eyes, come back and sit down in front of Kenny.

We start to talk, nothing much, just little bits, but easy enough. He's talking, I'm thinking, drifting away, thinking about Pam, thinking about Nan. Thinking about my brother.

I've never spoken to a blind man like this before. I've helped a few into the cab. All I said to them was,

"You OK? Watch your head" and they'd say "Yes." Then I'd pull the cab into the street, joining the other marauders of the day.

That was it. I'd never really sat and talked to one, had a

natter.

What was Lucy saying on the hill? I can't think. I'm in no state to think. And here I am with a blind man sat next to me in a pub.

It reminds me of my Nan, I came in with a paper for her when I was young, and she said, "I spoke to a Paki today." They'd just bought the local shop. She'd never spoken to one before, she was happy to have met one. And I'm happy to be sitting here next to Kenny, to be freed from my mind.

The pub starts to fill, lunchtime crowd, shoes and socks leaving desks, computers, phones. Some stare at Kenny when they come in, just a look. Just a look at the blind man look, but they don't want to be seen. They don't want to be rude. Mustn't be rude.

Kenny was given a bad set of eyes, any fool can see that. If it was the eyes or the pain in my gut, years with Pam waiting to be blown, torn away. I love her, love her with all my heart. Same with Gary, I'm going to lose the two? Then Lucy. Oh god, what a mess.

I look at Kenny see his teeth, dirty and black. Why should he care?

Chapter 7

"I was brought up in a home," he says, like he's been thinking about it, like it's all he's wanted to say. Like it's all been leading to this. Like a road that runs to the sea, he wants to talk.

"What, like a blind home, a place for the blind?"

"No, a regular children's home, my Mum and Dad were the wardens. We all lived there."

He tells me his story and it is a story. How his parents were wardens, wardens before they even wanted their own child. He was their accident, their little accident child. Being the warden's child he had his own room on the top floor, full of talking toys. His parents overcompensated for his lack of eyes. Every toy talked, parrots, penguins, they all made a noise with cords you had to pull. The orphans slept on the second floor in two big dorms, rows of beds, touching walls.

"I always felt spoilt, compared to the others. I knew I was. I got presents, I had a Mum, a Dad. I only ever got given presents in my room. My parents didn't want the other children to see. I was only allowed to bring one toy out at a time. That was the rule. The other boys never knew how many toys I had, I had a few. My friends never came up the stairs. Mum said everyone needed a little space."

He told his story, I lit his fags, no wonder he was turning his fingers brown, he smoked one after the other, taking them down.

"You can smoke." I said, wanting one of my own. He didn't hear, he just carried on with his story and I let him. Talking is what this Kenny boy wanted to do. Talking is what we all want to do. We've all got our little pains, our stories.

"One of the boys had an alcoholic Mum. I only ever saw her when she was drunk. This one Christmas she came in with a present in a bag. You could smell vomit as soon as she walked into the room.

"The woman was crying, saying things like I'm sorry, I'm sorry, I got it wrapped. I wanted you to have it wrapped. And the boy was crying, my Mum had to ask the woman to leave. But she wouldn't, she pushed Mum. Dad came in, and they carried her out. She was swearing, crying, and kicking at Mum and Dad. Saying things like 'I only wanted to be a good mother.' Simon, that was his name threw the bag on the floor. Shouted to his Mum's back,

" 'I don't want you coming here no more'. I don't want you ever coming back here again.'

"I remember Simon, he used to get picked on, he was small for his age. I don't think his Mum ever came back.

"That night my Mum unwrapped the present with the sick on. Cleaned the bear, put it at the end of his bed.

"My parents were firm but fair."

Kenny stops talking. I look at my pint then up at his slits.

"They sound nice," I say.

I don't even like the word nice. I don't know what else to say. I'm not comfortable when strangers tell me stories like that. They do it in the cab, rattle on, opening up, bits of them coming out, coming off, falling out into the air of the cab. All I've got in response is my nodding head. But on they go, to a nodding head. Kenny's doing it now, rocking, then he stops and says,

"Yeah, I think we got on well."

I light him another fag, he takes in, doesn't start to speak until the last bit's blown out. I look at the packet, I'm thinking what's the point of stopping anyway? Shit, I've got a blind man doing it in front of me, he ain't even scared. It's the devil's nicotine breath talking. Instead of having one, I spin the ashtray, with the name I don't know.

I should have one, go back to the flat with one in my mouth. That would show Pam something's wrong. She'd see the fire coming out. I'm going to ask her tonight, have you or have you not been fucking my brother? No, I'll ask Gary, no, I'll ask them together.

Kenny takes another hit of his cigarette, and I watch.

"One Sunday, after lunch, my Dad said 'I think I'll go sit in the other room, take a nap.'

"I was sitting in the corner of the room when Dad said it.

" 'Sure darling, I'll tidy up,' Mum said. Sunday was our day, the day for the family.

"So Dad got up from the table, took himself off for a nap. Went into his room and closed the door.

"That's the last thing my Dad ever said, 'I think I'll go take a nap'."

Kenny stops, rocks, I light him another fag. He's on number seven, all sticking out at angles in the ashtray, ash on top.

"He had a heart attack, died with one hit. Died on his favourite chair. Didn't even have the time to know he had a dicky heart. Just boom and gone."

I say "I'm sorry about that." And I am. But he doesn't hear me, Kenny just goes on.

"Then on the Wednesday my Mum fell down the stairs, carrying a basket of sheets. She had it piled so high she couldn't see over the top. She slipped and fell. The doctor said she hadn't even broken her neck, she'd done her spleen. I was at school."

What's a spleen? I'm not going to ask him that.

Then he stops. I cough, I don't know what to say, so I keep quiet.

Kenny rocks, then stops.

"In four days my life was changed, just like that."

He smiles. I don't know if he's shaking his head, or if it's just rocking. I'm looking at him. That's a hard thing to happen to a blind man, hard thing to happen even if you could see. He's not talking now.

I take a sip from my beer and say,

"How old were you when all this happened?"

"Fifteen."

"Young." I say, thinking about me at fifteen, living in my head. Walking streets with my imagination for company. At fifteen I was a child with long legs. I never dreamt I'd be a doctor. Do doctors dream of being doctors, when they're young? Maybe they do.

"What?"

I look at him, I'm back to talking out loud.

Kenny's quiet, I've got to talk, I don't want to try and out trump him, lay my ace high story. Anyway I don't have one, I've never lost two people in one week.

"I lost two goldfish before Christmas day was out," I say. Kenny laughs.

"Is that right?"

"Yeah, alive in the morning, dead in the evening. I reckon Mum got some dodgy ones."

It's a lie, but it's the first thing that came into my head. We drink our beers, the barman reads his magazine.

Kenny says, "I had no next of kin. No aunties, they'd died years earlier. I remember my aunt Helen pushing a boy through a shop window once. I'd knocked into his arm. The boy turned and told me to watch where I was going. I heard all this glass breaking, and my aunt laughing. She got off with a warning because of me being blind. Mum and Dad wouldn't let her take me shopping after that.

"I ended up living in the orphanage, even though I was blind. I was only a few months away from my birthday, they thought it would be the fairest thing to do. Let me stay on at the orphanage. So it wouldn't upset my exams."

I nod my head. He sucks his fag, blows out the smoke. Then continues.

"They moved me down from the top floor, to the dorms. The new warden was trying to be nice, he wanted to give me a hand, his daughter was going to get my room. He told me he knew just how I felt.

" 'Please, let me help you with your stuff,' he said.

"But it was something I wanted to do on my own, I didn't care if I fell.

" 'I'd rather do it on my own.'

"He didn't help after that. And I bounced the boxes down the stairs."

And Kenny stops talking.

None of this shit happened to me. Well not then, I guess I'm in my own pile now. Nothing really, just a wife and a brother at it.

Kenny then says,

"I unpacked all my old toys, dumped them on my new bed, I was too old for them. The other kids were all at school, the room was empty, quiet. I'd been given time off, I was having a bad week.

"I split the toys up, walked them round the room, dropping

them onto other beds. When they came back from school, they looked at me sitting on my bed. I could feel their eyes. One of them said,

" 'We don't want these, you have them back.'

"And each of them walked them over, put them at the foot of my bed. Even the young kids, who didn't have much, they walked them back."

And then he finished.

What do I say to that? He's a man with a story.

"That must have been hard." I knew it was bad before it was out of my mouth. But how can you stop something you don't even know is on its way out. That's the trouble with words. So that's what I say to him after he's just told me that, "That must have been hard."

"I became one of the boys. An orphan in my own home."

This time I shake my head, but he wouldn't have seen that.

I look at him, he's rocking, maybe it's what gave him the rock.

When someone tells you something like that, you've got to give something back.

"Want another drink?" I say.

"Yeah, sure."

I lean over, pick up his glass. The barman serves the drinks, he doesn't want to. But he does it, and I thank him, thank him for pouring my drink.

I put the drinks onto the mats. Then say,

"I don't feel so fucking great myself." I don't want it to come out like that, but that's how it comes out. I don't know why I even said it. Kenny looks at me with his eyes that don't work, doesn't say a word. Just rocks, and a puff on his fag. Puff the magic dragon.

"What do you do?" Kenny says.

"A ferry man, a circler, a mover in black. I drive a cab, black taxi."

"What's that like?"

"It puts you three feet away from everyone you meet. They talk, you listen, and then they're gone. That's about it. I could go on."

Kenny looks at me.

"You must hear some shit. I hear some shit, being blind."

"Oh, I hear some and pick up fools."

Kenny leans his head back and says,

"Any women in yet?"

I look around the room. He's got a thing about girls.

"Who is it you're looking for?" He's obsessed. What is it about men and women?

"Anyone who'll have me." He grins, rocks. He's on the pull, fucking Kenny's on the pull. And I haven't had a pain in my gut for a pint and a half.

There's a few in for lunch. Smiling, talking. I don't think they're waiting for a blind orphan to come over and talk. I don't tell him that. What I do say is, "there are some having lunch."

"Whereabouts?"

"The other side of the bar."

"You push me in their direction I'll smell them out."

He grins. I look at him, I don't know if he's joking or not. He hasn't any eyes to read.

"They're by the fruit machine, can you hear it?"

He's probably got better ears than me.

Someone's playing on it, the wheels are going round. If he had eyes he'd see the cherries, pears, and bright lights, spinning round and around. And the man with the gut resting one hand on top, and the other pushing the black buttons to make it spin. I've got eyes for that.

"I hear it."

He gets up.

"Do you want a hand?"

"I've got my stick, I can hear the machine. And then I've got my nose."

I look at him, as he walks the carpeted space to the machine. He gets close to the girls having lunch. His stick hits a chair. The girls look up, smile, then go back to eating. One looks at him for a little longer, then she stops looking as well. None are rude and none show any interest in him.

Kenny comes back with his stick.

"They're not my type." he says.

So he knows his type. I thought I did.

"Oh right, and how do you know that?" How does he know that?

"She's waiting for a call. Can you help me find a phone?"

"Sure, there's one on the counter, over there."

Who's waiting for a call? What's he on about now?

I point, forget he's blind. I realise what I've done. I look at the barman to see if he's seen me point, but he's still reading, he wouldn't see a thing, not unless it was with other Aussies from the back of a van. Kenny says,

"I'm looking for a booth?"

"Oh, right. You got a phone card?"

"No, but I'd like a booth."

"Sure."

He knows what he likes. I help him with his coat. Hand him his stick. The Australian carries on wiping. He must have wiped every glass in the pub and now he's on his second round.

We walk across the floor towards the half-glassed door. I walk at his pace, like walking with a child. When we get to the girls' table, he stops for a moment. They're talking, I can't smell a thing. One's swearing, the others are laughing. Kenny doesn't say a word. I get to the door, pull it and hold it open. His stick leaves first, followed by him, then me.

Outside the day's brighter than the pub, even got a little shine in it. The bag of grey snot, which has been hanging over us for a week, has moved on, left some blue.

"Do you notice any difference, you know, day from night, outside from in?"

"Not a thing. Makes no difference to me. And day always turns to night. My Dad always used to tell me off for not turning off the lights. I told him a light to me is just a click of a switch. When I told him that, he said he was sorry, he never told me off again. He was trying to save money on electricity. I don't have to worry about that, my light bills are low."

I laugh.

"It's true." He says.

His stick's swinging out wide, I'm looking for a red telephone box. A man walks past, wiping his brow. A police car sits tight on the side of the kerb, inside two white shirted policemen eat out of a Kentucky box, they're not moving until they've munched that box. They look like good eaters. They smile as we walk past. I smile back, I doubt if Kenny even knows they are there.

I find him his red box.

I help him with the door. He squeezes past me, lets his cigarette drop to the floor, he doesn't bother putting it out, it just smokes away at our feet.

"I'll close the door, alright?" But he puts his stick out, so the door won't shut, it's trapped in the door.

"Are there any cards in here?" he says.

"Cards?"

"Calling cards, spankers and wankers. Girls, doing what they do."

He laughs, looks at me, then starts to rock.

I once came out of a library, it was cold, I put my hat on. An older man came out and did exactly the same. Then turned, smiled and said,

'Us men are lucky we wear woolly hats, women have those things which point out in front.'

I think that was his reasoning as to why women get cold and men don't. He smiled, wished me goodnight.

Kenny's looking at me with his nappy rash eyes.

"Oh, calling cards. Yeah, loads," I say.

Some people collect them, I've got a friend who's got them all over his toilet door. He goes in there with his phone. I can't take Lucy there.

"Then I'm in the right place. Any green ones?" Kenny says.

"What, do you collect them?"

Maybe he needs a green one for the set.

"No."

The booth's covered in them. Little ones, big ones, women advertising what they do.

"You're lucky the council didn't get in here first," I say, looking for his green lady on a card. Red and black seem to be the colours.

"Lot of red ones here, Kenny, you thought about maybe red?"

I don't like looking for things, I'm no good at it.

All the policemen eating their chicken have to do is look up. We can be the first job they do after lunch. Come and talk to the blind man and his friend who are hanging around looking at cards in a booth.

"No, green's the colour for me."

"Hey, hhhey, there's a green one here, I've found your card."

There's a green one stuck above his head. A lady with a whip, in black plastic gear. I pull it down and have a look.

"Why green?" I ask, as I hand him the card, but his hand isn't out, so the card waits in the air.

"Here," I say again. This time he raises his hand, I put the lady with whip into it.

"Because I'm green with envy, green with pain, no, only joking. I like walking over grass, it's nice under my feet. I like the smell of cut grass. I've been told grass is green, so

I've always had a soft spot for the colour green. Started when I was young."

"Grass isn't green, who told you that?"

I laugh, he laughs. Me and him laughing together.

"Is it green?" he says. I don't know whether he's joking.

"Yes, it is. So do you dream in colour?"

"I've never seen a colour in my life, they've been described to me, but I've never seen one. I dream of smells, dead animals that sort of thing. I hate milk, my Dad made me drink too much."

"You hate milk?"

"I hate milk so I hate the colour white. I'd never choose white. Don't even like to wear a white shirt."

I don't know whether he's joking, but I laugh.

"Can you dial the number?" Kenny says, tapping the lady and the whip, smiling up at me.

One of the officers gets out of the car, carrying his eaten box, he's walking straight towards us, but stops at the bin, puts his carton in. Then wipes his lips on his shirt sleeve.

"Excuse me then Kenny."

He moves to the side. I take the card from his hand, push the numbers for his date. Wait till I hear someone pick up the phone, it's a woman, I put the phone to Kenny's ear, he holds it. I go out under his arm.

"Thanks," Kenny says, "Will you wait?"

I nod my head, then I say, "Sure."

I stand outside, while he talks. I don't know, I don't know. It comes out loud, a man, walking past, turns, looks at me.

Looks at me as if he's waiting for the answer. I've got no answer to give, but being outside makes me think about me. My problems, what the fuck's going on?

Kenny's talking, happy on the phone.

I'd stopped for a drink and now I'm doing this. Chance, fate, call it what you like, things happen, they always do. As day turns to night.

The Soho chatter and clatter goes past, happy suits, carrying whatever they carry under arms. Shoes in a hurry to walk, ready for their next shine. Deals being done on phones, smiles and glances, so happy, London town. Kenny's voice is loud. I turn. His nappy rash eyes moving up and down, fingers twitching in and out. Fingers like a bird after its been thrown from the nest. Twittering, twittering fingers, moving slits.

Then he rocks, she must be talking back. I stop watching.

A limo comes up the street, pig, big and ugly. Three blonde heads popping through the roof, like corks going off. They're smiling at each other, one's taking pictures, the other two waving back. They're too old to have blonde heads popping out a roof. I'm too old to be blonde. They wave as they go past and I wave back. Like a lot of things I do, I have no idea why I waved back.

Kenny taps on the window, his eyes are as red as the box. He's finished. He's having trouble with the phone, he drops it and it swings from its cord.

"Sorted?" I say, as I pull open the door.

"Yeah, all done, you don't know where D'arbly Street is do you?"

"I know it, I'll walk you there, it's not that far."

I know every street, every crack, years spent staring at a

map, mopedding round the city with a board out front.

We walk up the street. Past hairdressers snipping, women and men trying on coats. We're in the cartoonist's, film maker's, ideas world. All the ideas in their eyes, in their heads, bright people, who like to let you know, from the comfort of the back seat. Sometimes they even say," You seem too bright to be driving a cab."

I thank them very much, continue with my driving, not wanting to put them, their face into a post.

"You ever wonder what you're walking past?"

Kenny keeps walking, then says,

"I listen. I'm listening now. If I didn't have ears I'd be trapped. These things are what keep me alive." He taps an ear. "Without these I'm as good as dead."

"So what do you hear now?"

"You. I heard clippers back there. People walking, talking about things they're going to do. You know, that sort of thing."

I nod my head. Sometimes you get on with people and you don't know why. Others you just smell them, know you never will. It could be the hair, the eyes, the voice, but you know you'll never get on with them.

"You know what you're walking past, as good an idea as me, I drive past this shit all day. It takes a shower when I get home to wash it off." And it does, soap dissolving the slime.

When he walks he doesn't rock. People get out of his way, it's like he's got a flashing light on his head.

"You clear a path."

"Yeah I do, I don't always want to, though."

We carry on walking at Kenny's pace.

"Where d'you live, Kenny?"

"Mottingham. You know it?"

"Shit, I live in Deptford, Mottingham in Kent right? Not far from me."

"Yeah, South London boy, hey."

He says back to me, then he looks up, so I look up, I don't see anything there.

"Neighbours, near as damn it. I'm staying with my Nan in Sidcup at the moment, looking after her for a couple of days."

"Why, is she ill?"

"No, she's just lost her husband. She's finding it hard."

"I'm sorry about that."

He stops walking when he says it. I think he wants me to know that he means it.

"It's OK, she's old, these things happen."

He must know all about that. He doesn't say anything else, just carries on swinging his stick nice and wide, so I don't say anything back. It keeps things simple.

I'm looking at him, his stick, thinking about what he's just about to do. "Isn't it a bit dodgy, you know, going with a prostitute?"

"I trust her voice, she's got a familiar sounding voice. A voice you can trust."

Chapter 8

I've never been to a prostitute. Never wanted to use a woman that way. I've taken them home after they've done their shift. Lots of them, driving them home in their battered, layed silence. Just sitting on the back seat, sucking and blowing on their cigarettes. The ones I let smoke, that is. Some I wouldn't let smoke, they're too far gone. Too drugged up on whatever they're on, wouldn't know whether they were holding a fag, a dick or a conversation. Prostitutes have these eyes. Kenny wouldn't know that. He's saved from their eyes. I asked this one once, it was the second time I'd picked her up, she wouldn't have known. I asked how she got into it.

She looked at me, her eyes meeting mine. I didn't think she was going to say anything, so I got on with the driving and the night. Then from the darkness of the back she said.

"I asked Mum if I could kill my hamster. I thought if I killed it, it wouldn't have the chance to run off, wouldn't leave me, like my Dad. Mum looked at me. I'd never seen her look that way before. She said 'Come here darling.' You know how Mums do, in that nice soft way. So I walked over and she took my hand. Then with her free hand she slowly stroked my face, touched me under the chin, slapped me over and over again. 'Wicked girl, you wicked girl.' My Mum screamed." Then she stopped talking.

I didn't ask her anything else, didn't really know what she meant, just took her home.

Prostitutes' eyes are tired, eyes that have seen too much.

Late at night bouncing along, them sitting in darkness, me sitting up front. It's just a woman going home for a wash, to put powder where cocks have been. Tired and used up, they don't want a man. They want an empty bed. They have a hard life.

I picked up this old silver haired one once. That's what you do on the darker side of midnight. We got talking, I didn't have to ask her what she did. She knew, I knew. She was talking and I asked her what it was like? She didn't say anything for a while and then said.

"The first day I did it, there was this old girl, don't know how old, but old. And she says, this is a job where you die young, it's either your spirit or your mind. I don't take drugs any more, just pain killers to keep it all numb."

All the prostitutes I've driven home, I felt sorry for every one. Even the bad ones.

Last week a man asked, "You know a good knocking shop, drive?" They always ask, as if I should know.

"No, the one I used closed up. The girls were that good, they all got married. I even married one myself." As soon as I said it I felt cheap. Saying that to a stranger, this git in the back of my cab.

It satisfied him, he gave me a nod. Then he sat there with that what-am-I-going-to-do-with-my-dick stare, but he left me alone. I like to be left alone, up front in my mind, driving bridges, listening to the night. Turning the wheels, finding the next finger to put on my seat. The same night I got another rat, things come in threes, I was at Victoria station and he wanted to go to the Isle of Dogs. A New Yorker, he ate pussy, lots of it. He loved talking about it. That was all he talked about from the moment he got in. Telling me what and how he likes to eat. He wanted to know if I get to eat a lot of pussy in the cab? What's my favourite type? What smell gets me hard? He would rather eat pussy than fuck, drink beer or watch TV. He's desperate for pussy, lots of it, and on and on he went, with his tie straining at his American neck. He got out on the Isle of Dogs and the last thing he said to me "Go get yourself some pussy and eat it." Gave me a goodbye wink.

He wasn't drunk, just a man with a hobby, and a one-year contract.

And my own brother's in my home doing the same.

I'm walking a blind man down a street to do something I've never done. I've been truly put off.

He's probably done loads of things I haven't done. I wouldn't have put this on the list. I'm walking with a man ready to deposit his load. I bet not one of these avoiding his nappy eyes types would put a bet on that? They wouldn't be thinking that, as they smile, looking at his stick and getting on with their days.

Kenny says,

"What you want me to do? I can't look in the yellow pages, I'm lazy with Braille. I've already told you, my Mum's dead. Maybe she would have taken me."

Have I've been speaking out loud?

Then he laughs. Just a little laugh, a laugh all the same. He turns to me, shows me the red slits I guess he calls eyes.

"I wasn't judging you," I say.

"I couldn't care if you were." He stops, I stop. "You don't have to come with me, just tell me the way." He says it in that quick, that's the end of that, sort of way.

"I'll walk you there, it's only round the corner. To tell you the truth I haven't anything better to do, I'm avoiding my day."

He touches his eyebrow with his finger. We walk the rest of the way in silence. I don't know what he's thinking, I'm listening to him and his tapping stick.

We come to the door, one of the numbers is loose, hanging on by one screw.

I turn and say. "Make sure you don't get ripped off."

Some prostitutes want to swap what's on the meter for a bit

of mouth, bit of head. They've lost their way, used up, no heart.

"I'll do it for what's on the meter," this one girl once said.

I looked at her in the back, our eyes meeting in the mirror, I slowly shook my head. She didn't care, she was just making me an offer.

I hope Kenny gets one with a heart.

"I've done it before," he says.

"I'm sure you have."

Kenny's feeling around for the buzzer, long fingers moving up, down, trying to hit the buzzer, trying to let himself in. He's finding it hard.

"Up a bit," I say. He's getting near, but he's not on.

His finger moves up, he hits the buzzer, waits a second then pushes it again. After the third time he waits. I wait by his side. It crackles, then a woman's voice.

I should tell him about the bits in his teeth.

"Kenny?" I say.

"Yes."

He turns, I don't know him well enough, I don't know him at all. He looks at me. But it's Kenny who speaks.

"We can have another drink after if you want? Talk a little more."

"Sure, why not," I say.

The door phone's crackling. I push it, open it wide. Help him in. The stairs are long, steep, red and carpeted. Stairs you'd break your neck on if you were drunk, tumbling stairs.

"I'll give you hand, I'll get behind you."

"I'll be alright, I've climbed many stairs, many stairs on my own," Kenny says.

"Well I'm here now."

I put a hand on his back, he takes his first step.

"You smell that? That's woman." He smiles turning to me. I see the food wedged in his teeth. I can smell something, it doesn't smell like any woman I'd want to be with. Just something out of a cheap can.

When we get to the top, there's a blonde lady, fingers covered in plastic, big, thick, pink plastic rings. Like the crap you pull from a cracker. A thunderbird girl. Her hair's piled up on top, a bra showing under her shirt. I've taken plenty home, sitting under a used skirt in kissed out silence. She's got the look. Kenny can do what he likes and I see what I see. She would have seen some men climbing these stairs, and I would have taken a few of them home.

She says, "take your time, they're steep. Hello boys."

"Hello," Kenny says. Shit she thinks I'm here for it as well. Maybe she thinks I'm a helper.

"Come in." She holds a door open.

"Was that you who just rang?"

"Me," Kenny says with his rotten eyes.

"Good, so you know the score?"

"Yeah, that's fine."

And she's looking at his stick, his eyes. Looking at him.

"So what do you do, with such fine fingers?"

"I tune pianos," Kenny says.

There's a lot of lying done in these rooms, under sheets. "I'll just sort a few things out," she says.

I'd have no idea how old she was. She could be anywhere in the stream of life.

She leaves the room, we stand there not talking, standing in the middle of the room in silence not moving an inch. I let my eyes move around the room, but Kenny he just stands there. She comes back in, smiles, smells like crap.

"Ready?" she says.

"If you are?" Kenny says.

"Here, give me your hand. You can sit and wait." She says turning to me. Pointing to the split, peeling, cracked chair. The foam's coming out, someone's picked at it, pulled away at it while they waited.

"Thankyou," I say, take my red chair.

"Watch your foot on the rug. Here, give me your stick." And the piano tuner is led away.

The phone goes, the answer phone takes the message. It's another man wanting to do business. I wish Gary could have come here. That's all he had to do, get himself off the sofa and out the door, down to a place like this.

I wait and then they're finished just like that. I hear the door open, slow, shuffling feet. I'll give it to him Kenny's got balls. I open my eyes, he's there with the woman. His shirt untucked, she's the same, standing and smiling.

"Here, have my card, you never know when you might need it next," Thunderwoman says to Kenny. I don't know why I call her that, but I like making up names for people, it's what I do. I couldn't intellectualise about it, can't even describe why.

Kenny puts his hand out, but she puts the card straight in

his pocket.

"I've put it in your pocket love."

Kenny drops his hand. "Thanks again," he says.

"Anything for you?" she says.

"No I'll be fine, I'm doing alright. I've got a wife," I say giving her a look.

"I see a lot of men who do," she says.

"Yeah, honestly, I'll be fine."

I get up, go to Kenny's side, lead him away, down the stairs. Slowly we go down.

"Thanks for waiting," Kenny says into the back of my ear.

When I get to the bottom, I turn round, watch him take the last step. The woman's smiling at the top, she waves, with a fag in her mouth. It must be the worst thing about her job, all that time without a fag.

"Come back whenever you want." She waves with the money in her hand.

And Kenny stops, says over his shoulder.

"I might well do that."

"Keep the card," she says.

"I will."

Kenny pats his pocket.

She buzzes the door, and out we go.

Chapter 9

The day's trying to be bright, but the clouds are ganging up, it's turning from blue to grey.

"Do you fancy that drink?" Kenny says, while I'm looking up at the sky. I nod my head. Then say, "Why not?"

"Good. We can talk some more."

"Funny, I keep nodding at you," I say, and I do.

"You can smile and nod, do what you like, I don't care" says Kenny, smiling, taking me by the arm. Slowly we walk down the street. I'd never noticed how fast I normally walk. People move out into the road, avoiding his stick. We go past the phone box, then the Kentucky carton in the bin, the colonel's head poking out. Back to the pub's half-glassed, print marked, booted wooden door.

We go in, it's all the same. The Australian, no friendlier, still reading his magazine.

I have a coke, I've stopped on beer. Kenny, he sticks with the beer.

"Did you smell that dead bird?" Kenny says, with his cigarette burning.

"Dead bird?"

Kenny then says, "yeah, dead on the pavement or the road. It stunk, it's got a particular smell."

"We didn't walk over anyone who was dead. I would have noticed."

Is he rocking or shaking his head? I look at him.

"No, bird. Birds. The things that fly. Well I think they do."

"Oh, tweet tweet birds."

Kenny puts yet another fag out, laughs then says,

"There was something there. I can smell death, it has it's own smell."

He's smoking, his fingers are turning brown. He'll find out soon enough, if he doesn't pack that in, I think, congratulating myself on yet another moment of not having one, but I know I'm going to crack.

"Birds scare me, have since I was a child. One got in our class, the teacher couldn't get it out. I could hear this mad thing flying past. It's wings beating, trying to get out. It couldn't. It clipped my ears," Kenny says.

I think he's stopped, but he hasn't, just wants another hit on his fag. I watch him as he takes it all the way in, I wonder if I smoked like that.

Kenny goes on. "I had my arms over my head, I could still hear it. The thing was going berserk. The teacher shouting, telling us to remain calm. He wouldn't have known how to spell the word. Kids were crying, and it was getting louder, more frantic. Then there was a crash above me, then nothing. Silence. Something hit my head. I froze, it slid into my lap, flapping. I was worried about it's beak. I put my hands down, flicked it to the floor. But it didn't hit the floor, it landed on my shoe.

"I put my hand up but the teacher ignored me. He was trying to calm everything down.

"Slowly the bird died. I knew when it was dead. I smelt it straight away. I smelt death that day."

Then he stops, goes back to what he does when he's not talking. Rocks and lights another fag.

"Funny, I was brought up on birds, Grandad had a shed full, or aviary as he called it."

"You wouldn't get me in there. The noise, the smell." Kenny shakes his head. "No way."

I look at Kenny, I'm glad I met him today. He's taking my mind off my problems. And birds do have a particular smell.

"My Grandad used to race pigeons, used to strap them with a note. First one back, that sort of thing. A whole shed full," I say.

"I've heard about them, what are they called? Pigeon fanciers, a funny name," Kenny says with his sore eyes. Sore and red, I look at them again. I've been looking at them a lot. He's never even seen his own eyes.

"Yeah, on weekends he'd cycle them out, maybe twenty miles, more. In a basket on the front of his bike, with a dynamo going round. I'd go with him if I got up early enough. I wasn't good at getting up. He had hens, cocks, they all had names. One was called Julius Caesar. He'd take them off his bike, drop the basket and open her up. The pigeons would fly. They'd all go up and turn at the same time. Start to make their way home."

Kenny's nodding so I go on.

"They always looked like they'd been waiting for their weekend trip. It didn't matter how fast Grandad's dynamo went they'd always beat him. Be sitting on the roof cooing when he got home. He'd put his hand out and Julius Caesar would fly down, sit on his hand."

Kenny nods, then says,

"You haven't asked me what the woman was like?"

I hadn't asked, I don't want to know. But he wants to talk about it. He doesn't want to hear about Grandad's birds.

"Well, what was she like?"

"You don't really care. It's in your voice, Nick," Kenny says.

I don't.

I don't need to know what another man's woman's like. I can get that most nights out the back of the cab. Two men together, give them time, give them a drink, give them a lift home, it all comes out.

"I'll tell you a story," Kenny says.

"What, another one?"

Kenny laughs. "Yeah, another one."

He rocks, he's thinking. The pub's still half full. The Australian looks at us, I look back at him.

"She smelled and sounded fine," Kenny says.

"I'm very glad she did."

I am glad she was clean and had a nice voice.

Kenny lights another cigarette using the end of the one in his hand. He coughs, then says,

"The first time I ever touched a girl was on my sixteenth birthday. Elizabeth, the new warden's daughter. We'd got on from day one. She looked after me, helped me with things. It was the first time a girl had ever been like that with me. She felt sorry for me, I guess. She was a day younger than me. On weekends she'd take me out, go shopping, she was my escape from the home. Anyway on my birthday she took my hand, said

'I'm going to take you somewhere.'

She took me behind this shed. And when we were there she said

'I wanted to get you a present, but I didn't have time.'

I look at Kenny. How old is he? Not much younger than me. He takes in some more smoke, lets it out.

"I could hear her undoing her buttons, and she took my hand

and put it on her bra. I'd never done anything like it before. Then she undid my jeans, my penis stuck out and she got on her knees. It was the first time a skirt had ever sounded like that.

'Happy birthday,' she said.

"Then she started to blow, I didn't want that candle to ever go out. I wouldn't let her stop, I had a hand on her head, the candle blowing in the breeze. And that's what we did. We'd go down to that shed once a week and she'd blow my candle. Wouldn't touch, or suck, just blow on it, warm breath."

He takes another lug, I scratch my face. He blows the smoke out and goes on. I'm glad he's going on, because I don't know what to say.

"That's how it started. We'd go every Wednesday after that. And one thing led to another. One time she said,

" 'I smell different after we do this. You can smell me if you want but don't touch.'

"I nodded my head and got on my hands and knees. Smelled her, moved my nose around her skirt.

"We got caught in the end. Her Dad came round the back. It was in his voice, he wanted to hit me, but he couldn't, so he said,

" 'You dirty little...'

"He couldn't say what he really wanted to say, but it was there in his voice. I didn't know who he was speaking to. Elizabeth ran off. Then he said, 'I'll be watching you.' He had a big voice and he gave me a poke in the chest. I lost my balance. He was talking to me this time. He made that very clear.

"I had to find my own way back from the shed. I fell over. The warden was near, he didn't help me get up. The last two years in the home were hard. In a busy room I wouldn't know where he was. I always thought he was looking at me.

"He stopped his daughter from eating with us at weekends after that. Banished her to her room.

"She used to play the violin, in her room, my old room. I'd sit on the bed, the bow dancing across the strings. I felt every note. She told me what the violin looked like, I held it in my hands. Then it all stopped.

"I wasn't allowed in her room anymore. Not after the warden caught us."

Kenny stops, has some beer. I'm just about to say something when he goes on.

"On the weekends, when we were having lunch, I'd hear the violin. I forget the piece now, Mahler maybe. I thought she was playing the music for me. That's what I thought. I never got the chance to ask.

"One day her Dad said from the head of the table.

" 'I can't stand this anymore.'

"He pushed his chair away from the table, it made that screeching noise. The room went quiet. There were only a few of us there, the younger boys and me. I thought his footsteps were coming to get me. But he didn't come to me. He walked upstairs and the violin stopped. I never did hear that violin again. And I only ever had the chance to speak to Elizabeth once more."

Kenny stops talking.

It's another one of his stories. He's had a life this Kenny, more than I would ever know.

Chapter 10

I'm swinging in and out, trying to catch waves of lights. I'm in my black office, driving to the beat. If you get it right you can get a run on greens. Not a red one to be seen. It saves tap dancing on the pedals, not moving to the brake. Kenny's rocking away in the back. He says,

"I didn't realise I was blind till I was eight. I thought everyone else was like me. I'd never been told."

"We're all blind Kenny, one way or the other, all of us," I say. I don't know if he hears.

I look at him in the mirror. His eyes are staring outside, he's got a hand against the glass and he can't see a thing.

I say loudly, so he can hear,

"You're going along the Embankment. We're on the north side and then we're going to cross the river, go over Tower Bridge. Years ago the prols could pay to see the King eat his Sunday lunch in the tower. He might have a deer, a pig and a cow. More, if he was hungry. You had to buy tickets though, otherwise you weren't allowed in. Or if that wasn't your fancy you could watch a polar bear on a chain, go fishing in the Thames. Maybe watch a hanging in the afternoon. The Tower was where it was at. You could spend all day there, you'd never get bored."

Kenny keeps rocking.

The Thames is on our right, the sky's going from grey to night. I should smile more. I've got sad lines on my cheeks. I noticed the other night. I was sitting at lights, caught my mouth in my mirror. I told myself to cheer up. That night I smiled whenever I could.

I follow brake lights, cut myself in and out, slowly cross the bridge.

"You're on the bridge now," I say.

Kenny speaks, looking out his window.

"You're not a bad driver, there's no honking going on. Sometimes I get these drivers, it's deafening inside. What's this, diesel?"

"Yeah, you ever been in a cab before?"

There's plenty in London who haven't. Minicab people, cheap with their lives. It's an insult I give to people when they're up from Croydon, and we've left the only street they know. And a little voice from the back says, "Where are we now?" And I say to them, "What, did you know where you were a minute ago?"

I'd forgotten about Kenny, I was on a rant. I can do that, go into a rant. Do it most days. That and talking out loud. But I'm safe in the cab, they don't hear a thing. I'm in the partitioned box.

"No, never," Kenny says. "I feel a car, then smell the fuel, oil, the rubber. I've never been in one of these before."

"First time for everything."

Then I think about what I've said. Its getting dark, he wouldn't even see that.

Then he says from the back, "To me a car's a door. Something you get in and out of, that's all it is. A door. Cars vibrate, noisy really."

I drive on, he vibrates in the back, then he says,

"What's driving a cab like? Ever worried you might get mugged? You hear about it on TV."

"I don't worry about it, I keep my twenties in my boots."

"I'll remember that," Kenny says.

"Driving a cab makes you dizzy. You're going everywhere and

97

nowhere. I make 0800 calls, when I'm bored. I rang one the other day, it was about losing weight.

"This woman was talking, saying things like, 'well with this product,' and 'if you stick to a regime.'

"I was listening, she was talking. Then she said 'any questions'?

"I said 'Yeah, I got a question, I've got two stone to shift, got to lose it by Friday, I'm going to a party. How am I going to shift it?' She didn't say a thing.

" 'You listening to me? Hey? How am I going to lose the weight?'

"Then the line went dead. Killed a minute on a set of slow filter lights. Made me smile."

Kenny nods his head, says,

"I could do a bit of that myself." He is a bit fat. But why the fuck should he worry about that. Women had stopped looking at me years ago.

Then we stop talking, drive in silence.

I look at him in the mirror. I think about Glad sitting in her chair, waiting, waiting for the box to be lowered, Bert's cross to be drawn. Sadness just blew in.

Glad's got this Chinese fortune cookie in a cabinet in her flat. Been there years. On the white card underneath it says,

'Your marriage will be full of love.'

She got it at a restaurant. She wouldn't eat it, she wrapped it, put it in her pocket. I remember Grandad leaning over, saying,

"Here mother, have half of mine."

I was only five but I remember it.

He'd call her mother sometimes. She smiled, took it from his hand. On the way out, the waiter gave me a bag of prawn crackers. Nan walked with her cookie and her bit of fate.

It's still sitting in her cabinet now.

It's going to be hard for her, I'm only just getting over my Dad.

She never got on with my Dad. She'd say things like,

"He's got two sides to him, the side when he's smiling, the side when he ain't. I don't trust the side when he ain't."

She's full of them.

"Your Mum would come round here, when you were young, chunks missing from her face."

His death's going to be hard for her. And how long have Pam and Gary been at it? When did that start? Behind my back, my brother and his smiles, the pain in the gut kicks in.

There's a buzzing in the back. It's a bee, Kenny's trying to get it with his hand.

"You reckon you could stop, help me with this bee?" he says.

I pull the cab over, press the hazards. Get in the back. It's on a window. I open the door, it takes the breeze and leaves.

"That's the worst thing about being blind, having to ask people to do things like that."

The hazards up front keep ticking, the taxi waits at the curb, and Kenny goes on.

"I once got something in my eye, didn't know what it was, anyway I had my dog with me, Taverner. I had to get this thing out of my eye, it was cutting in. But I couldn't get it out with my finger, so I had to stop someone. I asked this man if he could help get whatever it was out of my eye, or at least tell me what it was.

"And he said' 'What me? No mate, I can't do that. I'm sorry, I can't'. He ran off. I swear I heard his footsteps running off. Taverner even barked, and Taverner doesn't bark."

"I wouldn't like to put a finger in your eye, Kenny."

"Yeah, but you'd be able to tell me if I had shit in it. Or would you run off?"

"Definitely run. Who's Taverner anyway?" I say.

"Who do you think he is? He's a fucking dog," Kenny says.

"So where's he now?"

"Dog's don't like escalators, not unless you carry them, and Taverner's getting old and fat. So when I come up to town I leave him at home, he gets a day off. But if I'd realised I was getting a lift home I'd have brought him. He'd have liked the ride."

"I don't allow dogs."

Kenny turns to me, rocks his head, then gives me this grin.

I don't say anything and he doesn't. We just sit next to each other on the back seat, with the evening traffic moving past. After a few minutes, I get back up front, push the hazards, pull the cab from the curb, join the others going home.

Night after night, nighters driving home. Driving in, driving home.

At least I'm going nowhere, I'm just going round and around. I wonder what it would spell if you etched into a map everywhere I'd been in a day. 'Help', it would probably say help, or 'my wife is a cheat'. It would say that.

"Help?" Kenny says. "Who do you want to help?"

"I was just thinking," I say.

"You think loud." Kenny laughs.

Chapter 11

We turn into his street, his Mottingham street. Redbrick land, fridges sleeping outside. Half bonnets, upturned cars. Forgotten carburettors waiting to be put back in. Cardboard flapping in the wind, where windows have been. Cans on walls, glass on floor. Guitars in windows, waiting, ready for that hard rock roar. I'm looking for his number, forty-four.

"Forty-four right?"

"Yeah, you coming in? Come and meet my wife."

I brake with my tap dancing foot, brake harder than I need to.

"Wife, you're fucking married then?"

"Sure, why not? Over four years now."

Kenny smiles.

He's married. I sit in my seat, he sits in his in the back. A blind cheat.

He says, "Give us a hand, otherwise I'm not going to be able to get out."

I turn the taxi off, flick the switch. Open my door and go and get him. He's lucky he's blind, I'm staring at him now. Married? I shake my head.

"Yeah, four years. Are you staring at me, Nick?"

I don't answer, I just say.

"Watch your head getting out."

"Shit." He hits it.

Then puts his feet on the pavement, straightens his back. There's a dog barking, it's coming from house forty-four. Its golden face at the window, there's a woman behind, on a chair. The light's on, she's sitting looking out the window.

I don't want to go in. I don't want to have to smile, I don't want to lie. Not that I can't, I just don't want to lie.

"I've had a good day Kenny. I've enjoyed it, we'll have to meet again. I better get going, I've got to see Glad."

I hold out my hand. He doesn't know it's there. He puts one step in front of the other, makes for his hanging gate.

"Come on, meet my family."

He says, then starts walking to the door. Oh so now I'm going to meet his family.

"Sure why not."

Some more thoughts got out.

His path's cracked, the fence is down. His neighbour's crap scattered around, blowing, rusting under the sky. There's a dog on a chain amongst the cans, it looks at us, then starts to froth.

"He's alright, he's an ex-pub guard dog. Grumpy old fuck. They say he's an alcoholic, he's a lot better after he's had a drink."

The dog growls, I hope the chain holds.

Kenny gets to door forty-four, his door, pulls out a key on a chain, un-clips the key, slides it into the lock.

The door opens, into a sliver of a hall. Not big enough for the two of us. I smile, Kenny's dog jumps at our feet.

"Down, Taverner, get down, boy," Kenny says.

Taverner's jumping, like any other dog, with its tail, swinging this way and that.

"Good blind dog," I say, and it's out.

"Blind dog? I've not heard him called that before."

105

Kenny says, laughing.

"I once asked this woman where such and such was. She bent down, and spoke to Taverner, told him where he should go. Left at the lights, then first right. And when she'd finished talking to him she stood up, and said to me,

" 'These dogs, they're so clever.'

"I laughed, what was I supposed to do?

"She said, 'Why are you laughing?'

"She had a well-spoken voice. I couldn't stop laughing and said. "He doesn't know where the shops are, you idiot, it's me you've got to tell."

" 'I don't believe you,' this woman said, turned and walked off."

I laugh, then he laughs, we laugh in his tight hall.

"Is that you Kenny? Kenny?" A woman's low voice from another room.

"Yeah, it's me love, I'm back."

Kenny puts his keys in a dish, then coins on top. Then empties his other pocket, puts the lady with the whip on top.

I look at him. I don't know.

"What don't you know, now?" Kenny says.

"Funny, my little Lucy asked me the other day what being blind was like and I said I hadn't a clue. And now I've met you," I say.

"After you," Kenny says, rocking his head towards the door. I look at him, then back at the woman with the whip, waiting to be seen. I turn, go through the door.

I walk in, there's a woman on a chair wearing blue. Her

hair's held up by a plastic grab. She doesn't look at me, she's looking up at the ceiling.

"I've brought someone home, this is Nick," Kenny says from behind.

"Hi." I say, walking towards her. She doesn't move, there's another dog at her feet. Also golden, not as large. She doesn't get up.

"Hello, nice to meet you, I'm Helen," she says, she's chewing gum. There's a pack open on the side of her chair. Still she doesn't look at me.

"Take a seat, want a drink?" She makes a gesture with her hand. Kenny hasn't said a thing. Just stands behind me. She turns, I see her eyes, they don't move, they're milky and blue, like her dress. She stares. The dog gets up, she pats it. Helen looks at me with these eyes. She's got a button undone on her top.

"Would you like a drink?" She asked me that before.

"I'm fine thanks, I'm driving."

She looks up to the ceiling, nods her head.

Kenny walks over to his wife, leans, gives her a kiss.

"How was your birthday love?" Helen asks.

Now it's Kenny's birthday, and he's got a wife. I hope that hasn't come out. I think as I stand in the room.

"Great. Nick brought me home, he's a cab driver. Proper cab driver, drives a black cab."

"Is that right, thanks for that," Helen says, talking with a half-turned head. She turns to Kenny.

"Lizzie's already in bed, she was tired. I put her down early. She made you a birthday card, she wanted to give it to you.

It's on the table."

Now he's got a kid.

"I'll go up and give her kiss." Kenny says. Taverner follows him out the room.

I'm left with silence and what's on my mind.

There's a picture of a toddler on the wall, smiling, walking towards the camera, two retrievers behind.

Helen sits there with her head turned, she's listening to Kenny above. I hear his footsteps, we're not talking, the room's quiet. I feel awkward.

My eyes move around the room, there are toys and things. Then I see a stick by her chair, a harness for her dog. Oh fuck, she's blind too. Kenny's a blind man cheating on his blind wife.

Her eyes aren't like his. They're wide open, it's taken me all this time to realize that she doesn't blink.

I don't know.

"Sorry?" Helen says.

"What a lovely dog," I say.

"Yes, she is lovely, good temperament. Needs one in our house."

Helen strokes the dog, picks up one ear and drops it.

"Have you known Kenny long, he's never spoken about you?" she says, with her non-blinking eyes.

"No, we met today, in a pub."

"He likes to go out on his birthday. He says he goes to the British Museum, listens to tapes. Now I know he goes to the pub too."

She looks directly at me. I don't know her, I don't know him, and I'm not going to lie. I finger the card in my pocket.

"I met him in a pub, he hit me with his stick."

She laughs.

"He did," I say.

"The Lord Clyde, was it? He took me there once. I don't like crowded places, I can't hear people talk, I tend not to go anymore."

Kenny's coming down the stairs. He must keep his child awake, walking like that.

He comes into the room, Taverner behind.

"She's asleep, did you close her curtains, I forgot to check?"

"No I didn't love, I forgot," Helen says getting to her feet. This time it's her dog that goes out the door. Helen follows.

I look at Kenny, he lights a cigarette. When it's lit he inhales some, blows out his smoke.

The curtains aren't drawn, the alcoholic dog pulls on his chain, the streetlight shines in.

"That dog needs a drink," I say, looking at it through the window. It does, it's in a pool of froth, its tongue out.

"Yeah, sometimes I slip out and give it half a pint."

I look at Kenny as he smokes in the middle of the room.

"A wife and a child?"

"We've been together four years."

"And a child. How old?"

He nods his head. He's rocking then he stops.

"Yeah, a little girl, coming up for four, Lizzie. She's beautiful."

"That's a nice name. Well Kenny, I should be going."

I get to my feet.

"Write down your number, I'll give you a call. There should be some paper somewhere, have a look."

There's paper on the table, a crayon next to that. I walk to the table. Lizzie's picture's there. A matchstick man walking his dog. Lots of bright colours. It's got Happy Birthday Daddy written at the top.

"She's good at drawing, it's a lovely card."

"That's what her teachers say. What's she drawn?" Kenny says, walking over. He can't even see a picture his kid's drawn. I look at it.

"It's a matchstick man walking a dog, she's coloured the grass, and there's like a rainbow in the sky."

"What colour's the dog?" Kenny says.

"Yellow. So she can see?"

"Yeah, thank god, we were worried, but everything worked out fine."

"That's good. I've really got to go."

I pick up the pen. Do I write the number or not? I write my number, I say it out loud. I put it under the matchstick man walking his yellow dog.

"Give us a call whenever you like," I say.

"Sure, you could take me round, show me the sights. You must know London pretty well."

We walk out the room.

"Bye then," I shout up the stairs. Her dog comes to the top, then her.

"See ya, nice to have met you," she says with a smile.

I look at her, then at her dog.

I turn, open the front door. Walk outside, the neighbour's dog's given up barking, it's just panting in a pool of froth.

"Give him his drink Kenny."

"Yeah, I'll do that."

Kenny pulls the door half-shut behind him, leans forward, says.

"I want to be a good husband, I try, but as you know, it's hard."

I look at him, smile.

"I'll see you Kenny, give us a call."

"Sure, oh, do us a favour, is there much dog shit out here?"

"What?"

"Dog shit, we pay this boy to come round and pick it up. I'm sure he doesn't do it some days."

I look down, then look around.

"I can see a bit, nothing much."

"Good, he must have come round. I worry about Lizzie she sometimes walks in it."

"She's not the only one Kenny."

I touch him on the shoulder, turn, walk to the cab.

I put the key in the ignition, start the taxi up. Kenny's standing there, his wife's back in her chair. Staring at me or

111

whatever blind people do, when they're facing a window. I wave, then lower my hand. Pull the cab away, drive to Nan's.

I'm driving along thinking about Kenny, and what a day. How these things work. A blind man cheating on his wife, my wife cheating on me. Is the whole world at it? Cheats and liars. Then there's Glad, waiting in pain.

I stop at a set of reds. I look to my left there's a woman and a man in a Jag. I look again, she's got tears in her eyes. A husband or whoever he is, looking the other way. I stare. It looks like the end's come in the green Jag. They didn't think of that, when they were buying the car. That didn't come with the leather seats, the walnut dashboard. The holiday home in France.

The same with me, when my brother walked me down the aisle, raised his champagne glass and wished me luck.

I pull away from the lights, leave with stories in my head. I don't know? And there's no one there to answer.

Chapter 12

"I'm not coming home tonight, I'm staying at Glad's" I say into the phone. Fuck her.

"Sure darling, whatever's best," Pam says back in a quiet voice.

"Yeah, this is best," I say.

"You OK love? How's she coping?"

"Not well, pretty hard to lose a husband or a wife."

"It must be," Pam says.

"It is, so what have you got to tell me?"

"Oh, not now love, not on the phone, you go and sort out your Nan. I think you're great, doing this for Glad."

"I bet you do," I say and put down the phone. And then it rings, I don't answer it, just push the power button off. My nipples are on fire, the cold stuff she's sprayed on stopped working.

Nan can't sleep. I hear wailing from her room. Pacing feet. She wakes at this time. It's the time Bert died. She's asked her doctor what she can take. The doctor looked at her, then at me tonight and said,

"It might be something you have to live with for the rest of your life."

The doctor was young, being honest, Nan cried. Then said,

"What you've got nothing that'll crack the code?"

The doctor looked at me, for help. I couldn't give her any.

"I don't think I can, Mrs. Bacon, there's nothing in my bag for this."

And then the young doctor left, she couldn't get away quick enough. Her seven years training had come down to an old lady in a room, with her grandson, sitting in gloom.

I'm sitting on the spare bed, having a blow. Taking it in deep, holding it tight. Filling my brain and lungs. I kid myself I'm not having a cigarette.

Glad's in there, pacing and crying. I want to help, but I can't. I'm stuck to my bed, I smoke my blow, start to drift. I can't hold my thoughts until the end. I drop the butt in the cup, wait to fall asleep to my dreams, they haven't been so good of late. Not ones I'd like to share.

"Nick."

It's Glad from her room. I get up and walk into her's, she's lying face down, just hair on a pillow.

"You awake love?" I say.

"What do you think. I can't sleep. Come in and close the door."

I close the door. And she says into the pillow. "Thanks for staying Nick, I've got something to say. I'm sorry for not liking you when you was a kid."

"That's alright Nan. You like me now, don't you?" I squeeze her hand. I don't mind. I was Grandad's pet.

"Turn over love," I say. She turns, she's old and sad. I look at her and she looks at me. Then she says.

"Biddy's knitting jumpers for penguins now. Saw some programme about penguins being cold. I thought they were supposed to be, stupid fool."

I look at Nan. I'm stoned.

Biddy, oh Biddy, I remember, an old friend. She lives in a home, lost her leg to diabetes, her husband to age and drink.

115

I used to visit her when I was young. I liked her, she gave me sweets. I measured people by bags of sweets.

"Sorry Glad, what was that?" I was drifting.

"Biddy, she's knitting jumpers for penguins. Your Mum wants to put me in the same bloody home."

"Is she going to put numbers on the back?"

"No idea. Promise me you won't let your Mum put me in a home. I don't want to end in a home."

Mum's spoken about it. How the best thing for her might be a home, Pam and Gary thought it was a good idea too and I remember nodding my head.

"Mum doesn't want to put you in a home."

"She does. You promise me Nick?" She's looking at me, waiting for the answer.

"I won't." And I think of Dad and his card lying eyes.

Glad leans forward, puts a hand on my knee. Whispers but it's more of a shout.

"I see them in there, with nappies and shit. They can't even shit in peace, all those eyes watching. Some sleep with eyes open. You don't know if they're looking at you, or too scared to sleep. I don't want to end up in a home. Promise me?"

It's come down to promises you can't keep. Like promises at the turning of a new-year, promises at a wedding, promises made by a wife.

"Don't let me end in a home? They let you lay in your own shit, with bedsores. Then they come round at night, giving you god knows what. I know what goes on in places like that."

"You won't Nan, you won't end in a home."

I stroke her hand and she looks me in the eye.

"She's having you on, penguins don't need jumpers, Glad."

"I know that. She's never had anyone on in her life. She won't be talking to me again."

"Why's that?"

"I wasn't going to watch a fool knit a jumper for a penguin. I told her, if I'd listened to everything she'd said, we'd never have got on. And she always had the eye for Bert."

"What eye?"

"She had the eye, you know what bloody eye."

Oh I know all about that, how little you know, I think as I stand over her bed.

"So you told her, then?"

Glad looks at me. "I don't want to sit opposite a fool at my age."

"There's another friend gone," I say. But I don't know why I said it, I haven't come in her room to have a go. She's been going through them, either dying, or by way of her tongue.

"How's that job of yours?" she says, turning the subject on me.

My job, I think, one job leading to another, all the people looking the same. Blurred into the road, the street, the lights. The window shops and their panes. The white lines, the bitumen, the crud. Think Nick, think. I take a breath and say.

"I picked up this old woman and as she slowly got out she said, 'It's a nuisance being old, it really is.' Something like that. Anyway she had trouble getting out. She'd broken

117

her back. And it's happy hour and she might have a drink, she might not. Her husband flew flying boats until he got blown up. She told me all this on the way over. She liked to talk, Glad. Flying boats were my favourite in Battleships I told her. And she said, 'He would have liked that.' I don't know."

I stop talking, Nan's waiting for me to go on, but that's it, there's no more. As soon as that door's closed they're gone.

She doesn't say anything for a while, then says. "That's a nice thing to have said. You're good at your job." She believes in a working man.

Behind Nan there's a picture. Grandad, in a jumper, a golfing hat. He's on a runway just about to board a plane.

"What plane was that?" I'm sure I know, but I can't think. Glad looks at the picture. "That's the one we took from America."

They'd flown out for Grandad's eightieth. He'd always wanted to see the Wild West. That's what he called America, the Wild West. The first time I saw him after he got back, he said, "That's a life's dream come true, seeing the West." We'd all clubbed together to get them enough Yankee cash.

"And the signatures, whose are they?" The photo's covered in them. Squiggles all over the plane.

They like names, Bert and Glad, they've got a dead list on the fridge, getting longer by the year. All the people they've ever known who are now gone. Bert started it off in thick marker pen. Now he's gone, it's up to Glad to continue it along. And when she dies I'm going to unscrew the fridge door, shove it in the back of the cab and give it a ride home. Hang it on my wall, get myself a thick marker pen and keep it rolling along.

"Other passengers on the plane. Everyone signed it." I stop thinking about the fridge.

"You got everyone to sign it?" I look at her.

"Everyone, I walked down the aisles."

"Why'd you do that?"

She's not looking at me when she says "Bert wanted to, you know he liked things signed. He loved that cowboy trip. The only thing that surprised him was that Indians drove Fords and didn't throw tomahawks. It was the best thing he'd ever done. Even got the Indian on his arm tattooed in again. I sat there whilst he had it done."

I hadn't looked at his Indian in years. Never even walked back to our tree with him. Time, where does it go?

I touch her blue, vein-pumping hand. It's rough, not like my turning the wheel, taking the tip hand.

"You've got stronger hands than me."

"What's the use of a hand, if you ain't got a hand to hold."

I think about not having a hand to hold.

"All the love in the world can't bring him back. Every night since he's been gone, I say, 'Now then Glad, you ain't going to cry.' And every night since he's gone I wake and cry. I miss him, Nick." She looks away, then says, "I never knew loneliness could be like this." I look at her, her old age, my Nan.

"Move over love."

She does and I get in beside her, and pull the covers on top. "Give us your hand." Our feet touch, and she passes me her hand. We lay in silence.

"Just don't fart," I say to her. She looks me in the eye and laughs.

I've got piles, they've changed the way I fart. The ointments don't work, I scratch them.

"Any suggestions for piles?"

"Use a hot poker," Glad says. And I laugh.

"You ever had them?"

"I've had everything. Even pulled a pig out of a canal."

"What?" I know I'm stoned. "What you say?"

"Course I did, you wouldn't let a pig float by. We was hungry. Had to kill it first. My brother did that, Benny, ended up in a trench. That's him by the plate."

She's pointing to the picture in front of the plate. A boy in an army uniform. Benny, smiling under a soldier's hat, waiting for his fate.

"That's him before he went off to die."

I look at the picture. "How old was he, when he died?"

She looks at me, then the picture. "Nineteen. I'll always remember the knock on the door. This man telling me my brother was dead. I was knackered before I got out of childhood. I've lived four of Benny's lives."

She shakes her head, and her hair lands on my face. I spit it out. She likes to talk about the old times, the time when she was alive. Memories and borrowed time is what she's got.

"After Benny died, Mum died in the last birthing of a head. I became the oldest of eight, even tried to put the new one on my breast. It didn't work, so I asked one of the others to find a cow."

That's her story. She's full of them. You just have to get on the loop.

"Mum paid good money to get that photo done." I look at Benny, then the plate.

"Those Royals should stand for a week, day and night, not just sodding Remembrance Day. All week in the middle of the bloody road, come rain or shine. Even if they did that, they'd owe us more."

She stops talking, starts doing something with her teeth. They come from times when false was better than your own. She takes them out, rattles her gums and puts them back in.

"That's disgusting," I say.

"What is?" she says, looking at me.

"Talking about our Royals like that." And she laughs. It's good to hear her laugh. Glad worked as a scrubber, scrubbed on her hands and knees all her life, with her arse in the air. Hospital wards, lifting and lugging. Worked till she was sixty-five, could have quit at sixty, but carried on scrubbing on her hands and knees. Every cup, sheet and plate in the flat's been begged, borrowed or stolen from the hospital where she worked.

And slowly I drift to sleep, me next to my Nan.

Chapter 13

Glad's snoring, her mouth's open wide, she woke me up. What am I doing in her bed? I get out of her bed and go and hang my black tie round my neck, and make myself a cup of tea.

When I'm done, I go into Glad's, she's sitting on her bed. All in black, with a gold cross out for the day. I've never seen it before. I stroke her freckled, ringed, hand. She's sitting in tears. They're dropping onto her gold crossed neck. Down onto her dress. I wipe away a crumb, flick another from her breast.

"Did you sleep alright love?"

She doesn't answer, I kiss her on the head. She doesn't want me there, she's preparing for the day. The day they never talked about, the one when her pigeon didn't come back.

People start to arrive. I lead them into her living room. It starts to fill, darkening with black cloth, the room's getting smaller, the air thin. In a row we sit, with people I know, people I don't. Facing each other. Smiles that don't know whether they should appear. Silence, what's to say?

We sit twitching, moving crossed feet. And then from the door "Would anyone like a cup of tea?" Mum says. Eyes look up. People say, "Yes please."

Pam and Gary come in, little Lucy in front. Pam sees me, her eyes widen, she's noticed my hair. Brown to blonde. Lucy comes and sits on my lap and stares at Glad by the fire.

"Nana's crying," she says in my ear.

"I know," I whisper back.

"Daddy you hair's changed." And she touches it, like maybe

it will come off in her hands.

Pam comes over. "You alright love?" She's looking at my hair. She goes to touch it. I move my head back, this ain't no time to talk, to be touched. Gary's at the door, he's seen me as well and his eyes are laughing, even though there's no noise. He's laughing at me, so sure in his suit. Poncing at my house, fucking my wife, you think I don't know. Oh, I know.

Nan cries and we go drop Bert in the cheapest box from page three.

Lucy's getting used to seeing grown-ups in black. We buried my Dad last year.

"You're the same as me now, Daddy," Lucy says as we lower the box. I look down at her, with a tear in my eye. Then we turn, walk away, with bent heads and heavy backs, our shined shoes out for the day.

"They'll meet again now won't they, my Grandad and yours?" Lucy says. "Maybe watch a cowboy film together." Then she buries her head.

"Hey, I met two blind dogs yesterday." I don't want to hear her cry. Pam's by my side. Lucy looks up. "Blind dogs?"

"Sorry, guide dogs."

She loves a dog, spends hours looking at them in books. We won't get her one, though every day she asks.

"Really?" She takes her head away from my sleeve. "What were they like?"

"Retrievers."

"Long haired or short?"

"One was bigger than the other that's all I know."

"Oh Dad, next time look carefully."

Pam squeezes my hand. I look at her. I take my hand away from hers. I don't want her holding my hand here.

"Sure love, maybe next time you can come." I say looking at Lucy.

"Please, where do they live?"

"Not so far."

"I want to come if you see them again."

"I'll take you."

Then Lucy walks off, catches up with Gary, and puts her hand in his. He pats her on the head and she looks up at him. They start to talk, I can't hear, and I don't want to. I don't even want her holding his hand.

"Did you really?" Pam says. "Did you really meet some guide dogs?"

I look at her, nod my head. "Yeah, Pam, I met a blind man cheating on his wife, and their two dogs. Oh, and he had a kid."

Pam stops walking. "How'd you know that?"

"Because I took him there, and waited outside the door. Then I saw his wife, saw a picture of his kid."

Other mourners move past, we get in stride, follow their feet. And Pam, she moves a little away.

I drive, lead in the procession, with my family in the back. I look at them in the mirror, one eye, then on to the next. We drive our black line through traffic and arrive back at Glad's, for the chitter chatter. The wake, nice smiles, over bits of cake.

I'm talking to people I haven't seen in years, the how-are-you sort of talk. I ask about their families they ask about mine. Ping pong. All so very nice.

"Still driving a cab? How's your wife?" he says. "I haven't seen you in years."

I don't even know his name. "Oh fine," I say. " We're getting divorced, she just doesn't know it yet."

"I'm sorry about that. That's a shame," he says.

"Yes it is, I think she's fucking Gary. Do you know Gary? He's my older brother, look that's him over there." And I point to Gary who's taking a drink. Gary sees me looking at him and waves.

"That's him, see the cunt who's waving," I say.

"Right. Well nice seeing you again." He puts out his hand for me to shake. I shake it and then he's gone and I'm left on my square of carpet, alone.

Glad's in her chair, being kissed. These people haven't seen her in years and now they're kissing and crying with her. Holding her hand, looking at her eyes.

Then it's all over. The room goes from full to end of wake. People putting on black coats over black suits and dresses. Leaving with tears dropping to socks, saying long goodbyes.

Gary's sitting with Glad, the two G's, the sinner and the griever. I can't look at him. My own brother, with my wife.

I'm shaking so I take another drink, walk into the kitchen, Pam's got her hands in the sink, water and bubbles going round and round, she doesn't know I'm there. I watch and drink my drink. I don't know what to say.

"How long have you been there?" she says, as I pop another can and make her jump. She smiles at me, the smile I know and love, but no longer trust.

"Long enough to be watching you. But not long enough to

know. All those years and for what, hey Pam?"

"You look sad love, they had a good life together, they really did." She leaves the sink, comes walking to me. But I don't want her touching me so I move away.

"Come back love. Lets talk, I've got something I want to tell you." I leave her with her bubbled hands and a shake of my head.

Chapter 14

Mum's in the hall, she's aged in the last couple of years. Burying her husband now her Dad. They say death comes in threes. Everything comes in threes. Buses, luck, death, all coming along in threes.

Dad gave me my name. A Saints name. He came into the hospital just after Mum had me.

He'd been selling belts and buckles. It was the sixties and people wanted them, lots of them. People in those days didn't like to leave their belt hoops empty. He was doing well, and he thought 'What's another child? What's another child to a man who's doing well?'

As he comes into the ward, the nurse says,

"So then, what are you going to call him Mr Gibbs?"

My Dad stutters, looks at Mum, she has me on her nipple.

"I really don't know. Haven't a clue, this is my second," Daddy says.

But she's a matron.

"What no idea? This is your second child and you haven't got a name ready?"

"I don't. I don't have a name, I've been busy selling belts and buckles" He lifts up his shirt, points to his buckle. Dad liked to tell people what he did.

"Well Nicholas is a nice name, I called my last son Nicholas. And it's a religious name. Are you religious Mr Gibbs? Do you believe in the God Almighty?"

He wasn't.

"Yes, you bet I do. Now Nicholas, that's a nice name. Nice ring to it."

"So we'll call him Nicholas then? I've got a chart, to fill in," the nurse says.

"OK, that's a good idea. How about Nick as a name?" he says turning to Mum.

"Sure darling, whatever."

She didn't care, what with me suckling so well, taking the milk.

So I'm called Nick. And that's how the story of my name goes. We all have a story to our name. Matrons wouldn't be allowed to do that today.

We had Dad's wake, five months before he died, we knew he was on the way out, he'd been told, and they got it just about right. The food was cold and the chef had left, the waitress cried, cried at our table. Dad said, "Don't worry, love, take your time."

She smiled. We talked, in wicker peacock chairs, about what he wanted, what needed to be done.

"Your Mum's sorted. I've spoken to the accountant. She'll have enough money to see her through."

He went on, "And I don't want to be buried, I want to be burnt, nothing on."

"OK Dad," we both said at the same time.

"Why waste perfectly good clothes? Anyone tell me that?"

None of us could.

"Do you want any music Dad?"

"Give us some Burt Bacharach."

"Alright we'll play some Bacharach."

"And keep the service short."

"Sure."

"And wear some new shoes boys."

"Anything else?"

"Yeah, have a card game afterwards."

"OK." And that's what we did.

We took a photo, we all stood in a row and a stranger took the shot.

He went in naked. With his eyes open wide and turned to ash. I've got that picture on my dash board, it circles London with me.

Mum's tired she's picked up a shake, her smile's starting to slide. The one we have for others when we make out we're doing fine. I've got one now for Mum.

"Come here," I say and put her in my arms.

"We'll be alright, we'll manage won't we?" she says.

"Yeah, we'll be alright. I'll stay with her, you go home."

"You sure?" Mum says, turning. She loved her Dad. He loved her. That's all you needed to say about them. It was the way they talked, looked at each other. "Go home Mum. I'll take care of Nan."

Mother and daughter, blood and pain, a misunderstanding from birth. They've always clonked, never understood what the other meant.

"You make sure you get some sleep, you look tired," Mum says in her black dress.

"I am Mum. I'm tired and sad."

"I know love, I know."

She's already told me. It's the first thing she said outside church. It's the first thing she always says to me. It's what she says when she meets and leaves me.

I'll always be her child. I move my arm down her back. She's right I am tired. Too much time turning the wheel, thinking about Pam.

We walk, over the carpeted, crumbed, waked floor, to the front door. Feet grinding crumbs to dust.

"Thanks love."

I kiss Mum at the door, squeeze her hand, run my hand down her back, feel the clips of her bra.

I had a thing about Mum's bras when I was young. She liked the natural colour ones, ones that looked like skin.

When I was about ten, I went into her room, she was taking her bra off. One strap was already over an arm, the cup was hanging down. I thought something was wrong. I couldn't look, so I left the room. It wasn't until years later that she lost one. Maybe I knew.

It's raining outside, heavy, sad rain. Rain for Mum to walk with.

I open the door, the charms rattle. A horseshoe with spurs on top, nailed to the front door. A present bought on his last cowboy trip.

I look at them, wait for the spurs to stop spinning.

"I won't say goodbye to the others," Mum says. "I don't want Lucy to see me like this. And don't let Mum drink."

"Alright love." I close the door, on my Mum's departing back.

That's why I got guard duty tonight. Mum had come up to me after the funeral and said. "Nick, I can't stand it when she drinks."

She makes Mum edgy after the whisky's gone in. She can't take Glad's tongue.

Chapter 15

Nan's crying by the blue flamed fire. Her legs are open wide taking you to her stockings, then on up to her crutch. All hidden by a black hang-nail catching dress. Scotch, rattling in her filled cup. Her, me and the rattling cup. She swings the ice round and around. Her make-up's run.

A deer's horns look down on us. A yellow napkin at her feet, and a sausage on a plate. Gary comes in, winks at me. I don't wink back. Why the fuck am I going to wink at him? He has no idea, none, he's playing a game.

I pick up my drink, then the sausage, chew it up, move it around and around.

Nan's shaking, sipping her scotch on the rocks, looking into her glass. She talks with a high noon tongue, after she's had a few whiskies. Every film she's ever seen sits on the edge of that tongue.

I start to tip the wake into the bin, let paper cups, napkins slide in. Move around the room, dropping things into the bag.

"You're good boys," Nan says from her chair. She's moved closer to her box today. Old since I knew her, in her zippered feet.

"I always wondered what it would be like when he was gone. Now I know." Her eyes don't leave the cup.

"You alright bruv?" Gary says coming to my side.

He's fucking calling me bruv.

"I'll open the window Nan?" I don't answer him, and I move to the window.

She doesn't hear. Her hearing's going, her aid's set on one. It should be on three. But she gets a crackle at three, so she has it set on one and we shout.

"I'll open the window, Nan," I shout.

"Just fucking open it," Gary says raising his eyes to me as he says it.

"What, love?" Glad says. I point to the window.

"I'll open the window, let in some air."

She nods her head, goes back with her head to the floor.

The window's covered in prints, handprints where people were propped. I pick up a napkin, start with a huff then a turn of the wrist. Bring back the shine to the glass.
My life's no longer mine, I think as I look into the garden.

"Leave'em, one might be Bert's." Nan shouts from her chair, by her blue flamed, sucking the air, fire.

"Turn your aid to number three," Gary says.

"What?"

"Number three. Turn the fucking thing up, please." I point to her ear, then tap the back of mine. I shouldn't talk like that. I look at the prints, stop huffing, I've been told. I put the napkin in my pocket, pull out the funeral sheet of songs. Songs for Grandad's journey in his box. 'Onward, Christian Soldiers.'

"Hey Gary, you never sang the song." I noticed in the church, he didn't sing, I sang, he didn't.

"What was that Nick?" Glad says, Gary's looking at me, with a frown on his face.

"Gary never sang the song. Let's hear you sing it. You'd like that wouldn't you, Nan, Onward, Christian Soldiers?"

Glad nods her head, and I look at Gary.

"Come on son, I'll start you off. Glad wants you to sing." And I start to sing, in a menacing way. "Onward Christian soldiers marching as to war with the cross of Jesus going on before. Christ the royal master leads against the foe, forward into battle, see, his banners go."

And I'm singing it so loud Pam comes in with Lucy. They look at me.

"Come on, let's all sing the song," I say. Lucy comes over. "See, Lucy wants to sing." Pam looks at me. "Did you notice Pam, that Gary didn't sing in church?"

"No, no I didn't."

"You didn't notice, well I did, so let's all sing it now. How about it Gary? Let's belt it out, for Bert."

And he looks at me. "What's wrong mate?" he says.

Now I'm his mate?

"Bert won't be getting no Queen's card, will he?" Nan shouts, from the fire.

"Number three. For fuck's sake number three!" Gary shouts back. Nan goes back behind her ear. She's got another card of sorrow in her hand. She's spoken about it before. Sometimes I think she's spoken about everything before. She's on a loop. Just depends where you get on and where you get off. Her legs are still open wide, taking you up to her crutch.

"You might make it. What is it? A hundred? How many years you got to go?" Gary says.

"Eight," she shouts. I walk from the window, get behind her ear, do some mechanical work, turn the switch to three.

"What you doing behind my ear," she shouts.

"Sorting things bloody out," I say.

She shakes her head, takes my finger from her ear.

"So many cards, I didn't know so many people cared. Kinder

than me own family."

"People care, don't they Gary? We all care, we're family right? We're brothers right?" I say taking off my jacket, putting it over the chair.

"Whatever you say," Gary says back.

I bend to the fire, turn the greasy knob. The flames dip then die. There's a china dog by the fire.

"You ever taken that dog for a walk, it looks overweight?" I say.

"Never, it's china you fool."

Lucy comes over and strokes it.

Glad won it, on some Blackpool trip. Shoved so many two pees down a shoving slot throat, that eventually the thing gave way, flashed its lights. That's Nan's idea of having fun. A place by the sea, with holes to put money in. Under lights, with all that fizzing, humming, candy floss noise. I spent years with her, winning crap.

"How will I ever sleep again?" Nan says. "You will." And she will, under a haze of pills and booze. Mum asked me to slip one in her drink.

"You'll get to sleep Glad, don't you worry about that. How you sleeping Gary?"

"I'm OK."

"You're OK, oh that's nice, and you Pam? You sleeping well?" I've got to stop, I owe it to Lucy, I've got keep myself together. Pam looks at me, gives a little shake of the head.

"It went OK today, didn't it?" Glad says it like a child. Wanting us to agree.

"Fine, the funeral went fine," I say touching her leg. Her legs are strong, made for carrying potatoes, legs built to lift a sack. I look at my tap dancing taxi feet. Modern man.

"Your Mum never liked the service. She told me in the church," she says, looking me in the eye.

"She didn't mean it," Gary says, before I can come up with anything.

I look into the garden. Everything's cold, Grandad's bike turning to moss. It's a crying day, rain hitting the floor, bouncing back up. Grandad's shed, waiting for him to come open the door.

He won't be doing that, I think as I stare.

"Have his birds been fed?"

Glad doesn't answer, I don't ask again. I look at his shed. That's where they are.

Nan's talking to her cards again, she's got one in her hand. "Only last month Mrs Cox said 'You two aren't still alive?' And Bert, quick as a wink says 'we haven't fallen in the sea yet.'"

She nods at the card. Puts it back with the others on the shelf. She looks up at her lucky horns, things are either lucky or not in her book. The horns are lucky. Grandad got them from a deer in the park, it had died of old age. Bert buried the deer during the day, dug it up at night and took the antlers from its head. They've been on a wall as long as I can remember.

"Grandad did a good scalping job, what'd you think Gary? Took his head of nicely. You ever thought of taking anyone's head off?"

Gary looks at the horns. "Yeah." Then he looks at me. I turn from him and look at Glad. She's turning into a ghost already. Flames, bouncing in her eyes.

"He's fallen into the sea now," Glad says, gives her head another shake. The tears come again.

"Sea?" Lucy says.

Pam looks at her, and says, "It's just an expression."

"I'll spend another night with you. Pam can go home with Gary, can't you Pam? She'll like that," I say looking at Glad then turning my eyes on Pam.

"Sure I can love." And Pam comes over to Glad. Glad sits rubbing her feet up and down on the carpet.

"We can go out for breakfast, my treat." She loves a breakfast, the bacon, the egg.

"So so many cards." She's still on about the cards.

"He was a good man, a good policeman," I say.

"He didn't give a toss about that," Glad says with whisky on her tongue. She's paddling down on a river of tears, every time she looks at a card, it reminds her of him. I turn, look at Pam and Gary and all I see is durex deception. Nan looks at me then at Gary.

"Your Grandad loved his pigeons boys. My pigeon won't be coming back. He'd see his birds before he'd kiss me," Glad says shaking her head.

"When were you last kissed Gary?" I say, swinging my head at him, giving myself a little loppy smile. "When did you last put your tongue in?"

"No idea, what's it to you?" he says. He can do that, cut you off, he's always thought that he's so strong.

"I kissed you last night," Pam says smiling at me, talking to Gary.

"Yeah, I bet you fucking did," I say. In our bed, tongues going in and out.

"Nick." And Pam nods her head in Lucy's direction.

Glad looks at me. Then out to Bert's shed, my eyes follow behind. He'd sit amongst feeders and bowls, running his fingers through their wings. They'd fly down and sit on his head. He wouldn't move a thing apart from his hand, stroking a bird, the smoke coming from his mouth. He'd tell me it was his first cigarette of the day, the one with his birds.

"You want a whisky Nan? Me, I could do with a drink," I say.

She's still looking at the shed. That's her drink, a cheap whisky on the rocks.

"Please."

She holds out her cup. I pour the whisky, drop the ice from a height. The whisky spills out over the side.

"Put more in than that," she says. I look at her, then pour some more. And she keeps looking at me.

"What you done to your hair?" she says pointing, as I hand her the drink. She hadn't even noticed last night.

"What you've only just noticed?" I say.

"I'd have worn a veil if I'd had that done," Glad says. And gives herself a sip of her drink.

She's right.

"I've had it cut and coloured, love. What do you think? I thought Pam might like it?" I turn to Pam. She hadn't mentioned it, just gave me an odd look when she saw me today.

"What d'ya want to muck around with your hair for? It'll fall out soon enough." She leans forward, shows me her scalp.

"Well what do you all think then?" I do this little twirl. "Taken years off me, eh? You reckon it's taken years off me, Gary?" And I jump in the air, give my feet a heel click.

"Makes you look like a twat," Gary says. Pam laughs.

"Why did you have it done, love?" Pam says coming over to my side.

"I like it Daddy, I think it's trendy," Lucy says.

"Thanks darling." She'll look after me, she'll be there.

"Sidcup's full of used up high heels," Nan says looking into the floor. She's spent years shuffling up and down the streets.

"I've always thought Sidcup sounds ill, sick, sick in Siccup" I say.

"Bert used to say, this place had men behind blue cans. Tattoos with no hope, eyes long gone." She takes her whisky on the rocks, opens her red-lipped mouth, slides some in. Finishes it off with a crunch of the ice. "Teeth, they give you trouble when they're coming, trouble when they're going. You remember that Lucy." Then she crunches more ice.

"Yes Nan," Lucy says with her arms wrapped around my legs.

"Do you remember when I lost my first tooth?" I say.

"No," Glad says.

"It was in your garden."

"I can't remember that, I can't remember a thing."

She can when she wants. She has this selective memory, remembers things from years ago, forgets who's just knocked on her door.

"I was outside playing, I ran straight into the washing line.

Took my tooth straight out. You said 'put it under your pillow when you get home, a fairy will come.' Funny the things you remember, the things you forget."

Glad raises her eyes behind her glasses. "Did the tooth fairy come?"

"It never came. I'd forgotten to tell Mum."

"I bet you cried," Nan says.

"I probably did."

"Oh, you would have." And then she laughs.

"That's right Glad," Gary says. And they both look at each other, them against me. I did cry when the fairy didn't come. I'll take this lot on, one by one.

"Why didn't the fairy come?" Lucy says.

"I don't know now, I can't remember."

"My fairy comes," Lucy says.

"I know darling," Pam says.

Nan looks at me. "I saw people today, I haven't seen in years. I know shopkeepers better than my own family." Pam nods her head, Glad shakes hers. She's right, I mean to come, but I don't. And after a couple of nights on night watch I'll be gone, and she'll sit with her movies and birds locked in the shed.

"I'm sorry Nan," I say, and Lucy takes Pam's hand.

"Family, it's a strong word. But I don't think it means what it did," she says and nods her head.

"What do you think about that Gary? About family being a strong word?"

"It never helped me with my wife," he says.

"But it has with mine," I say.

"Yeah, I guess it has," he says, then we stop talking. The room goes quiet. They do when you stop talking, left with noises in your head.

Glad pushes herself off the chair, walks to the TV. Behind are videos, racks of them. Burt Lancasters, Robert Mitchums, John Waynes, Steve McQueens. All the guns and holsters you'd ever need. They loved watching a man with a gun on a horse, riding along.

I'd watch them on rainy Sundays, sitting at their feet. People getting shot in the corner of the room. Buffalos, Indians running from the screen. Hollering, waiting for the next kill. They were mean, tooting times. I loved it, sitting there as the guns fired and blazed. Glad would do sandwiches on a plate, thick ones, hand squashed down. Eat your sandwich, watching Indians meet their fate.

"I'm going to watch a film" Nan says. She's got a video in her hand. She's already made up her mind, chosen what she wants to see.

"Sure Nan, what's it going to be?" Gary says. She doesn't answer.

Nan's strong, she once punched Grandad. One punch, down he went. I was watching, eating stolen fruit. Nan looked and said

"Help your Grandad up."

I held out my hand, Grandad winked as he stood up.

"She's a good woman, your Nan, strong as well."

He was proud of her. He walked the park that day with one black eye.

"What did Grandad think about your stealing?" I ask as I raise my Queen Mary's hospital cup.

"It was none of his business," Glad says, with the video in her hand. Glad looks at the floor then raises her head, and says to anyone who wants to listen. "You'll be happy to remember whatever you can at my age. The good, the bad. I'm sitting here, one foot in, one foot out. I'm neither in nor out of the ruddy box. Been like that for years. Don't get old, don't get sick, that's my advice to you. There isn't nothing left in old age, apart from the waiting going on."

I love it when she talks like that. Talks in bursts. Like some switch in her head's been flicked. Something switches her on, then it's off again. Nan coughs, puts down her rattling cup, stops and stares. She pushes the play button, the video turns tape.

Cowboys start to rustle up. Men jumping on horses, boots, spurs, digging in, reins held, flesh smacked. It's moving on time.

I look at her, she stares at the screen. The television's loud, she's back on number one. Soon the shooting starts, guns blazing into our eyes.

"Still into cowboy films then?" I shout. I haven't sat and watched one with her in years.

"I know what's going on in a cowboy film."

A trumpet blows from the TV. We all look at it. It's a man in blue with his lips open wide. I haven't spent this long with Nan in years. On the table by the door there's a small cup. I walk over to it.

"Excuse me, Gary." He's got his elbow on the table. I pick up the cup. It's got dust on it, I blow the dust. Engraved is Glad's name, a date 1967.

"What did you win?"

I say turning to her with the cup in my hand. Lucy comes over and takes the cup. Glad looks at the cup, then at me.

"No idea, I've never won no cup in my life."

I look back down at the cup. It's her name.

"It's got your name on it and a date, have a look." I turn it around, on the other side it says 1st. "You won."

"I've never won no ruddy cup."

Pam looks at me and mouths, "Don't bother." I put it back down and Gary picks it up, starts looking at it. She's got a cup with her name on, and she doesn't know how.

"You have the bloody cup," Nan says to Gary.

Nan's neighbour walks past the window, I know it's her neighbour, she's told me all about her. She got the flat when her Dad died. He rotted up top. Glad got the flies, then the smell. He was a bent-double man, twenty five years younger than Glad, but already old with pain.

The last time I saw him he had his face on the window. Lucy and I waved. He didn't wave back. Everyone knew he never waved back. He had arthritis, he couldn't move his hand quick enough. He might have waved, but by then you'd be long gone.

Glad said Bert found him with his head at the window. He'd been dead a while, but no one knew.

When Bert found him, he said "You better get some spray and call an ambulance."

Glad went and called an ambulance. Grandad started on the flies.

"Thirty, trying to look sixteen. Look at her, fat with love. They're always at it. Donkeys are quieter than them. Nothing but an ass and a mule."

"What's a mule?" Lucy asks.

"Ask your mother, she knows, so does Gary," I say.

Lucy turns round and Nan looks at the woman's parting bum.

Glad's got to have someone she doesn't like, puts the fire in her belly.

I look at the TV, watch the dust and blood rising, I was weaned on these.

Glad says, "She makes me red angry. Women aren't like men, they should have more heart. Two weeks without calling your Dad. Just a bum for sitting on. No use for anyone."

Glad turns from the window, back to the shooting on the screen.

"You can't blame her," Gary says.

"I can and I do. Remember, we all get old. Even the very young become old."

"Will I become old?" Lucy says.

"Not for a very long time," Pam says.

"But I'm quite old now, aren't I?"

"Yeah, you are love," Gary says from his seat. He's drunk.

Glad looks at me with her slippered feet, the video turns tape. The stagecoach pulled down, a woman's being made to undress. I think of Gary and Pam and wonder where they do it. Who goes on top?

The woman in the frilly dress is screaming to be saved. A cavalry man charges in, gun drawn.

"There's some killing in this," I shout, I fire my fingers at the screen. "Bang, bang," I shout. "There's a lot of death in the world," I say.

"Lucy shouldn't be watching this," Pam says.

"It's a cowboy film, there's nothing wrong with it," I say.

"It's only a cowboy film," Lucy says repeating what I just said.

"No, come on, we should go now," Pam says, and she looks at me with her no nonsense eyes.

"I want to stay with Daddy." She gets closer to my leg.

"Not tonight." Pam's cross, cross because I contradicted her.

"Come on love, Mum's right. Are you alright to drive?" I say looking at Gary.

"I've drunk too much, I'm well over the limit," he says.

"Well there you go, what happened to all this swimming shit, getting fit?" I say.

Glad turns from the TV, looks at me. Her glasses are filthy. Spit, lard, or shit.

"Give us your glasses, love, I'll clean them."

She doesn't hear me, she's back into the shooting.

"Give us your glasses, Glad, it'll make the killing clearer," I shout.

She passes the glasses, I move them up and down my sleeve, shine them up. I pass them back, to her stretched, lined hand. She puts them on. I look at her zippered, slippered feet. Her ankles swollen and blue, with veins running through.

"Your feet are swollen"

"Too long standing, staring at the stone," she says.

And she was.

Nan looks at her feet. "When I was young my Dad used to say I had dancer's feet, look at these things now."

She stares down at them. It's been half an hour since she cried, she's going to start again.

I take her slippers off, rub her nylon feet. Her slippers will become extinct, the last ones in the basket in a cheap shopping mall. The clients are dying, the slippers will be burnt, the poison will rise, be gone. Nan looks at me, her silver dying hair, on top of her grey lined face. My Nan, I smile, I realise that I love her, just then.

"You know what, Nan?" But I don't say it, she'd cry.

The Indians are getting back on horses, riding off. Horses with swinging arse attitude follow, cowboys riding up top.

"Why do cowboys always win?" Lucy says, as another Indian hits the grass. Solider blue helps a lady off the floor. She smiles as he tips his gold rimmed acorn hat. The Indian lays dying, his stomach's turning red.

"Because the good are taken first." Glad says, as the gold on her wrist shakes, the teeth in her mouth click.

"So Grandad was better than you?" Lucy says.

Pam looks at Lucy then at me. "Don't be so rude," she says. A quietness hits the room.

Glad looks at Pam and says, "Leave the child alone. She didn't mean nothing by it." And Lucy doesn't even know what she's done wrong.

I look at the bird feeder stuck on the window. Lucy and I got it for them. We thought Grandad could train his birds to come to the window. Save his legs.

"Do birds still come and feed?" I say, changing the subject.

Glad takes her time to answer, she does in the end. "Yeah, they come, about the only things that do." She shakes her head and looks every one of us in the eye. We know.

"You reckon you could still ride a horse?" I say.

"They don't make horses anymore. I haven't seen one in years. Just fancy things which jump over poles."

"You remember that quote Nan? 'It takes seven years to become a doctor, ten to be a good judge and a lifetime to be a ploughman and plough a straight line.' Something like that." Nan was a ploughman's daughter.

"No," she says.

"Well you told me it," I say, and she did.

"No I never," Glad says.

"Maybe she's forgotten," Pam says. Glad looks back to the cowboys on the tape and says, "I've got nothing for old age. It's all a lie."

"What's a lie?" Lucy says.

"Old age, retirement. I've only a couple of funerals and maybe a Christmas left. That's it. All I think about is the past, and if I thought about tomorrow, I'd cry." She doesn't even know she's talking to a child, and if she does, she doesn't care anymore. I've heard it all before.

She looks over at her Welsh dresser, photos lined up in front of plates, people now dead, just names on their fridge door.

She gets up, walks slowly with her black, hunched back. Walks to the dresser, pulls open the bottom drawer. It gets stuck, it's neither in nor out.

"Here, I'll give you a hand," Gary says getting up. He's drunk, he's wobbly on his feet.

"I can do it," she shouts. "I can do it." Her back isn't made for bending anymore. She struggles with it and gets it open. Puts her hand in and takes something out.

"Here, have it," she says walking to me. It's Grandad's ashtray, a picture of a coal truck in the middle, carrying sacks of coal.

"Thanks Nan, but I don't smoke. I've given up," I say with a smile.

"Daddy isn't allowed to smoke anymore," Lucy says. She doesn't want me to. She's seen the anti advertising, made me feel guilty with every lug.

"He'll start again," Nan says, looking at me. "Every time Bert had one, I'd say, there's another nail for your tailored box. He smoked from when he was eleven, until his last night," she says with a smile.

"You won't, will you Daddy?"

I look at Lucy, I've got to do it for her.

"No love, I've had my last one," I say. And if only that was true.

"It's got ash in it, on the back of the truck, there's some ash," Lucy says.

"That was Bert's last one. No one's used it since. I put it in his drawer. You remember that elephant you made at school Gary?" Glad says looking at Gary. "That's in there." Glad points to the drawer, under her plates.

"You keep it Nan, for memories' sake," I say, holding out the truck with its coal.

"Have it. He'd want you to have it. When you start again, use his ashtray."

Grandad was the first man I smoked with. Me and Gary,

blowing smoke, with him and his birds.

"Have it, take it," Glad says again, with her outstretched hand.

"Thanks Nan," I say as she puts the ashtray into my hand and I'm left looking at the ash.

"Remember, you was his pet. You're like him and Gary's like me." And she winks at Gary.

"I'll remember," Gary says. I look at them both and Pam looks at me. It's all talk in the room now.

Glad says, "You see that holly bush, berries every year. Thick with berries."

I look out the window and by a rusting car, the spiky green leaves scratching into the roof lay bare.

"None this year, not one berry. At this time of year, it's thick," Glad says.

"Why's that?" Lucy says.

"I don't know, it means something. Everything means something. Even things which aren't said."

Does she know what I've been thinking?

We all stare at the bare bush. Maybe it knows Bert's gone, that he won't be coming along to cut and clip it. Would a bush know that?

Glad looks at me and says. "What you got under your shirt?"

"What?" I say.

She looks at me, points to my shirt.

I look at the TV, the cowboys are hunkering down. I don't want to look at my shirt. I know what she's talking about, I'm not going to look down. She's the only one who's noticed.

I look down, I don't want to but I do. The hoops sticking out of my shirt.

"Oh, they're nipple rings, Nan."

"Nipple rings, what the bloody hell are nipple rings?" And she laughs, and every one looks.

"Like earrings, Nan, but for your nips."

"Rings, for your tits? Why'd you want to put a ring through your tit? Do they clip on like my earrings?" she says. I start to sweat.

I look down at my shirt, I'd forgotten about them today. They're not as sore but they're showing like knockers on a church door.

"Well let's have a look then? Let's see," Glad says.

"Can I have a look Daddy?"

Pam's looking at me like I'm a freak, like she doesn't know the man she's been with all these years. Nan leans forward. She's ready to have a look. And Gary, well he just laughs.

I don't turn my head, I look straight at the TV. The man and the woman are behind the bush. All you can see is a boot and shoe.

I'm sweating, it's sliding down my back.

"There's a hanky in Bert's room," Nan says, pointing to the sweat on my head.

"You don't want to see my nipples, Nan." She will.

"I do. Teach this old dog another trick." And she laughs again. It's her second of the day. She's coming out from under her shroud, the whisky's taking hold. She's getting her late-in-the-day, whisky eyes.

"Go on Daddy, let me see," Lucy says.

"Yeah, come on." It's Pam, they're all having a go.

"I don't want to" I don't have any choice, this isn't going to stop til I raise my shirt. Glad's smiling, nodding her head. I lift my shirt, stand there, covering my face. Like a crispy duck in a Chinese window, I stand and wait.

Gary laughs first, then Glad, then the rest. Glad comes over and flicks at the ring on my tit. It bounces off my chest.

"Ow, that hurt," I say. It's red and sore.

"Hoop's are for bulls. You've got smaller nipples than Bert." Nan laughs again.

"Why the fuck did you get that done?" Gary says.

Pam looks at Gary, "Language," and nods at Lucy. She's already getting him trained up.

"What's it to you?" I say.

"Ohhh, touchy," he says.

Pam's still looking at me, "So what do you think?" I say.

"Bloody fool. Come on Lucy, let's go," Pam says walking to the door, with her hand out for Lucy to follow. She's had enough of me.

"I like it Daddy. Can I have my ears pierced?"

"No you can't, not until you're older," Pam says from the door.

"My friends do."

"Wait until you get older love, I think young girls who have it done look like tarts," I say.

"What's a tart?"

"Ask your Mum."

Gary and Pam are talking by the door.

"Have you told him yet?" I think I hear him ask Pam.

"No I haven't and now's not the right time," Pam says, leaving the room.

"Told me what?" I shout to her back, my head's under a light, the antler looking down on me. And I realise I'm still holding my shirt up, standing in the middle of the room. I lower it into my pants, tucking around my piles.

"What have you turned into, you ruddy fool?" Nan says, shaking her head, laughing once more.

"Nan, that's laugh number three. You know what, I think you're going to be OK. What's Pam got to tell me?" I say looking at Gary. Waiting.

But Glad's off. "What was you thinking, making yourself a beast. Nothing but a chicken or a bull."

I look at Nan and say, "I don't know."

"You're a funny one," she says with this little grin.

"Come on Lucy we're going now." Pam's got her coat on. She comes over to Glad and gives her a kiss, shakes her head at me. "Come on," she says looking at Lucy.

"Go on love," I say, bending down giving her a kiss. "How you going to get home?" I say looking up at Pam.

"Don't you worry about that, we will." I nod my head. "Bye then," I say again, but Pam doesn't wave from the door.

Chapter 16

Glad pulls herself out of the chair, gets to her old slippered, zippered feet. She's finished her whisky, the wagon train rolls on.

"Men lost their lives, so men can wear rings in their tits."

Glad says, shuffling to the TV, shaking her head, looking back at me.

"They didn't just die for that," Gary says.

"No, others died for less."

She's already making her way back to her faraway seat. Like a tugboat coming into dock. I watch her lower herself down. Me, Nan, Gary and ticking time.

The TV's loud. Cowboys galloping in the night sky. An arrow followed by a shot from the rocks, cowboys jump for cover.

It's getting dark. I put the lights on, eat a leftover egg.

"Want anything Nan, Gary?" I say with a sausage in my hand.

"Bert back." She says it with a smile, then shakes her head. I raise my eyes, put the sausage in my mouth.

"How about you Gary, you missing anyone?"

"No."

"Sure about that?"

He looks at me, raises the can to his mouth.

We're all quiet, Nan staring at the fire, me staring at her.

"What's the secret of a long life?" I say. I've always wondered. Nan looks at me, then down to the hoops creasing my shirt.

Nan takes her eyes from the fire and looks at me.

"Anger, anger will keep you alive. Like a Winchester, keep it oiled, so you're quick on the draw. Anger's the fuel, make sure you give yourself plenty to hate. And keep your eyes open wide."

Then she stops, looks at the ceiling above.

"I'll remember that," I say, looking at Gary.

Maybe it's the drink in me. Glad's staring at the flame in her four-legged chair, the antimacassar's fallen to the floor.

"So what do you hate? What's put the anger, the poison in you?" I say.

"There's plenty I hate."

She looks at me. You know not to cross Glad. She looks up, the music's thumping out.

I go over to the window, draw the curtain on the night.

"Might be a frost," I say.

"He'll be sleeping cold tonight," Glad says. And he will.

"You ready to try sleep? I'll do you a whisky on the rocks. One to take to bed?"

I'm going to drop one of those sleepers in. The ones Mum gave me, they're sitting in my pocket. Then I'm going to roll me a number, drop myself into a dark hole.

"That'll be nice, another whisky for the road." I thought she'd had enough. She hasn't. "I'm not tired, not tired at all," she says.

Music from upstairs, gunfire from Glad's TV and the sounds in my head. It's noisy.

I go into the kitchen, walk to the memorial fridge door. Look at the names. Names down to the floor, back up again. People they've known, now dead and gone. Dad's name on top of a Mrs. Sharp, her on top of Dorothy Burns.

I look at the names, some cowboys have made it to the door. John Wayne, Robert Mitchum. All hanging on the door. Some by cancer, others by old age, men, women, even a few by gun.

"Did you know all these people?" I shout from the kitchen, looking at the fridge door. She doesn't answer, so I go back in and ask her.

"Me and Bert, we knew them all."

"Even Julius Caesar, the pigeon's there and dogs you had."

Anything or anyone they've loved made it onto the door. If I die before Nan, I'll be on that swinging fridge door.

Bert's name's not on yet. A pen sits on top of the fridge. I pick it up, pull the lid, hold it in my hand. Bert's going under a Mr. James. In my best hand writing I mark his name on the door. When I'm done I step back. I put Albert instead of Bert. I could have used Pigeon, Dodge or Bert, these were all his names. For his journey to the sky, he's going with the name of Albert. I already want to change it to Bert, but the pen's made it's mark.

I pull open the door. It stinks, the world's gone off. All dumped in her fridge. Glad's from the time of no waste, when mould was as good as cheese. There's a dead ice cream splitting from its box. I poke at it. Things are forgotten inside her fridge. I get the last of the ice, throw the tray into the sink.

"You've decorated Nan," I shout. The walls are clean, white.

I'm talking to myself, Nan can't hear. There's too much shooting going on, the music from up top too.

I walk back into Nan, hand her the drink. Gary shakes his can. He can get that himself.

"You've painted your kitchen then?" I say to Glad.

She nods her head. "That was Bert done that." She's watching the TV, doesn't look at me when she says it. "He needed it all clean to write his story on the walls."

I look at her, she doesn't move.

"What?" What the fuck is she on about?

She turns.

"He started writing things on the walls. In one of them pens, that glow in the dark."

She turns back to the video, I can't see her eyes and it seems pretty normal to her. "What things?" I've been here at night, I've seen no writing on the walls. What the fuck is whisky woman talking about. "I didn't see any writing on the wall?" I have no idea what she's on about.

"Grandad started writing when he couldn't sleep. He started in the bathroom, worked his way round the house. He was worried he'd get Alzheimer's, forget the important bits of his life. He started it a couple of years ago."

She still seems more interested in the film.

"Why did he think he'd get Alzheimer's? Alzheimer's runs in families," Gary says, isn't he the bright one? He would have read that on one of his days off before dessert.

Glad pushes her lip out with her tongue and says.

"He knew a lady who walked her dog in the park. They'd talk most days."

"What woman? Look at me Glad, what woman? What are you talking about?"

Glad carries on. "This woman from the park, one day she tells Bert she reads tea leaves, and would he like her to read his. Bert being Bert, said sure. So she read his, that's what she saw."

"What did she see?" Gary says.

"That Bert should write down his life before it was too late, before he was too old. She made him promise that he would. He believed her. She knew other things about his life. Anyway he started writing on the walls."

I look at Glad and that seems fine by her. It seems as good a reason as any, why her husband would start writing on walls in the middle of the night.

Gary looks at me then at Glad and says, "Why not use paper and a pen?"

"This was his house, he could write where he liked," Glad says.

"Yeah Nan, but it's a bit odd writing on a wall, isn't it?"

"You're a fine one to talk, with those hoops through your tits." She points at my shirt.

They're still sticking out. What have I done? I've been drinking all day, I'm pissed. I don't know.

"What don't you know?" Gary says.

"What all this is about. Do you?"

"No idea," he says.

Glad says, "It's just writing on a wall. He said he'd leave me something to read. Did it most nights towards the end. He'd sit on a seat, write on the wall. I'd wake up and he'd be scribbling."

"So you just let him write on the wall?" Gary says.

"What else do you think we did at night?"

"Yeah Gary, what else do you think they'd get up to?"

He doesn't answer just shakes his head.

Glad points to the corner of the room. "There's some of it over there, where it looks bright."

"So wherever there's new paint, there's writing on the wall?" I say, starting to look closely.

"Pretty much so. It gave him something to do at night. That's when he wrote it. He had insomnia terrible." I don't know what to think.

Glad goes back to watching cowboys. The music's thumping from above.

"You read much of it yet?" I say.

Glad doesn't look at me but says, "I didn't have the heart to tell him, I haven't the eyes anymore. They hurt when I read, gives me a rotten headache. Bert knew he'd die before me, we talked about it. Men do the leaving, women the crying. He didn't want me to read it til he was gone. He made me promise. So he'll never know. He wanted to leave me something, a bit more of himself."

She takes off her glasses, rubs her sore red eyes.

"That's a nice thing to have done," Gary says, looking at the TV.

The cowboys have arrived at the fort. We all watch the door open wide.

"I'll read some to you if you like. No, I'll tell you what, Gary can, he's the one who passed his eleven plus," I say.

"I'm a bit pissed to read, you do it," he says.

"Don't tell me what to do," I say.

She still looks at the TV, but nods her head and says, "I'd like one of you to read it."

I nod mine back. "I'll read it," I say. "Big brother isn't up to it."

It's not every day you get to read your Grandad's writing on the wall.

"He said the first story's in the bathroom, after that I don't think it matters. You've got to leave a light on for a bit, then turn it off. It does something to the pen, that's what Bert told me."

"You haven't even looked?"

She gives this little laugh, closes her eyes and says, "He hasn't been long gone." I get up, leave her with Gary and the TV.

I walk into the bathroom and pull the cord. The light comes on, I stand and wait, nothing.

My mobile goes. It's in with Glad.

"Phone's ringing," Gary shouts.

I go in. Glad's staring at the phone, it's on the dresser, with the plates and photos. I pick it up, push the green button. Glad looks at me, shakes her head.

"Hello."

A man's voice. I don't recognize it, so I wait.

"Hello?" I say again.

"Hello, it's Kenny. Kenny from yesterday."

"Hello Kenny from yesterday, how do you do?" I laugh.

Glad looks at me and Gary carries on with his drink. There's shouting going on. I can hear a woman's voice but I can't hear him very well.

"Sorry? What?" I say.

"My wife wants to talk to you."

"What do you mean she wants to talk to me?"

"She doesn't believe me. What I did."

"What d'ya mean?" I stand there, my hand on my crotch.

"She wants to know where I went."

"Went?"

"Where I went yesterday? Tell her I went to the pub," he whispers.

And then I can't hear him, just shouting from behind. Glad looks at me, I look at her, move my hand from my crotch. The music up top pumps on.

"Yesterday," Kenny says again.

I can hear his wife's voice. She's yelling, calling him a liar and a cheat.

"Mum found his card, where you took him." It's a woman's voice, it's her, his blind wife.

I don't have time to answer, he's back on. "Can I come round? I've got to get out of here," Kenny says. I think that's what he says. "Can I come round?" He says it again. He's calling me, a man he hardly knows.

I shake my head, Glad still looks at me, but then she could be looking at my tits, the phone, my hair or where my hand's just been. I say into the phone. "I don't want to be rude but haven't you got any one else you can see?"

I realise I used the word see. Can't even use the word 'see' to a blind man.

"At this point you're the only friend I've got. It's her fucking Mum, she's never liked me," Kenny says.

"Jesus Christ," I say.

"What's that?" Kenny says.

Glad's still looking and Gary's joined in. I don't know what else to say.

"Is it alright?" Kenny says, the shouting's still going on.

"I'm with my Nan."

His wife's screaming at him. I hear "Liar, you cheat." She's crying little sobs, I can hear the sobs.

I can hear Rod Stewart from upstairs.

"Who's on the phone?" Glad shouts.

Kenny shouts, "Shut up." Then again "Liar, cheat."

"Bitch."

Rod Stewart's singing, 'Do you think I'm sexy?' through the wooden floor above. I imagine his hips going round, like the record he made.

"It's a friend, Nan. Kenny, I think he's in trouble. His wife's calling him a cheat, he's getting chucked out. Kicked out of home." And then I look at Gary and he's smiling at me.

"What the fuck you smiling at," I say looking at him.

"You seem to have got yourself in a state," he says. He thinks this is a joke.

"What's another stray, tell him to come round. I could do with the company," says Glad.

She swirls her drink, she must be pissed by now. I haven't given her that pill yet.

"Kenny? You there, Kenny?"

He is, he's fending off his wife by the sounds of it. He hasn't had time to put down the phone.

"OK, Kenny, you can come round," I shout into the phone.

"What?" Kenny says and then I give him the address.

"Did you get that, did you get my address? Do you want me to call a cab?"

"No I got it, I'll be fine."

"Sure?" Then the line goes dead.

"Is he coming round?" Nan asks from her chair.

"Yeah Nan, he's coming round."

"Who's Kenny?" Gary says.

"He's someone I met yesterday, while you were in bed."

So the blind man's coming round.

"Good, it'll be like old times, Bert always liked a night."

I nod my head. She doesn't care who comes round. So long as she doesn't sit on her own.

"Which one of you's going to read Bert's writing to me then?" Glad says, straightening her back, standing on her feet.

I'd forgotten about that. It's getting busy.

"I will, but I'm a bit pissed, Nan."

"Nothing wrong with being pissed. Bring us a chair when you come," Glad says, moving to the door.

"You want another drink?"

I don't know why I keep filling her up.

"Sure."

She always hears when I offer a drink. I never need to

shout.

I take a chair, put it outside the bathroom door. Glad sits, I get her next drink, pour one for myself.

"Here." I hand her the drink, she takes the glass, lifts it to her lipstick lip.

"Thanks Nick. I'll never forget this. How good you've both been to me."

"And where's mine, then?" Gary says.

"I didn't get you one, I forgot," I say. I didn't. He can get his own.

"Well thanks a lot." And Gary walks off to the fridge.

I go into the bathroom, turn off the light. Grandad's writing appears from the wall. It is his writing, his letters, his mark. I stare at the writing on the wall.

Shit, look at it. It's like some cave man's painting. Gary comes back with a can in his hand. "Shit," he says.

"Grandad turned into a cave man."

Glad stares at the wall. "Wait for that whirring to stop," Nan says. We wait for the fan to stop, looking at the wall. Fuck they're noisy.

It stops. I hear footsteps above. A pull of a chain and water going down a drain. It's the woman from upstairs relieving herself. Her piss going down the drain.

"It's that mule up top," Glad says, shaking her head. The music sounds even louder, Rod Stewart trying to hit the notes.

"Make sure you read it loud," Nan says. She's sitting by the door, a whisky in her hand, legs open wide, pants showing. Ready for Bert's writing on the wall.

"I'm not very good at reading out loud. I'm not very good at reading full stop," I say. I'm not.

"You're not bad, I've heard you read to Lucy," Gary says. He knows all about me. He's seen me sitting on her bed.

"Do the best you can," Glad says back to me.

I start.

Chapter 17

I'm not a believer I don't believe.

That's the first thing written on the wall. Then there's a cross. I look at Glad.

"What's he mean by that?" I say.

"He wasn't a believer in no Lord. He thought it was all bunk. He used to say those who go to church are nothing but lost sheep."

Nan knows, she nods her head, wants me to go on. Albert's writing is neat, like his writing on the fridge. I don't say anything, just look at his writing on the wall.

"Go on," Nan says. He's dated it. I go on.

February 14th

I kept birds all my life, I liked them. My father gave me his favourite one. I wanted to be like my father.

He was a miner, and when I came of age I followed him in, like all boys in those days did. It was dark and dangerous. I couldn't stand it, but I didn't want to upset my father. You had to know someone to get a job in the pit, it was a something to be called a miner in them days. Miners were the richest men I knew, when I was a child. So I did my job and followed him, on my hands and knees.

"Can you hear alright, love?"

Glad nods her head.

"She's alright," Gary says. I go on.

I never got used to it, I was frightened all the time, I couldn't get over the fear. Any sound down there made me jump. I stuck it for over a year. Men down there were as strong as oxes, pounding at the black gold. I always knew I had to leave, get away from my father and the pit. I never got used to it. I waited all day to get back to the surface.

I'd already lost an uncle in a pit fall. Father had lost friends with what started as a cough.

So this one day I come in to see him and he told me.

I know son. He said it without even looking at me. He was in with his birds. You've come to tell me that you're leaving, that you don't want to mine no more. It's in your eyes.

He sat there with his racing birds. Didn't look round. I sat in silence behind his back. He had seeds in his hands and he waited for the birds to come. They flew over and sat on his coal miner's hand. He turned and looked me in the eye and said slowly, so I got every word.

The only luxury I've ever had are these birds here in my hand and you my son. He hugged me. That's something I'll never forget.

But I'd made up my mind to leave and he knew it. I left my Mother with a kiss at the door. The men were walking past, ready for the day's work in the pit. Dad walked out the front door as usual then he turned and walked back to me. He pulled from his pocket his favourite bird, he looked at it, and then put it in my hand. I closed my hand over it. And Dad said. Send it back with a note. Don't forget your Mother.

I nodded my head and cried, he turned and walked to the pit.

I walked with that bird to the station and caught a train coming south. When I got to London I had to keep a watch on my bird. The people and smoke were thick. I'd never seen a city like this before. The dirt, the grime, worse than the pit. I wanted to get back on a train, and come on home.

I spent two nights under a bridge, but I knew I had to find some digs. I couldn't keep the bird in my pocket for long. If I let it out, it would take to the air and fly back home. I wasn't ready to send it back with a note just yet. I wanted to prove myself, I wanted them to be proud. So I left it tied in my pocket. I walked the streets looking for work. I walked and I walked, not knowing what direction I went. Over one bridge then back over another, all day I walked, in my boots, looking for work. I forgot about my father's favourite bird. And when it came to night I was tired, I dropped to the floor, the pigeon didn't move.

I didn't dare put my hand in my pocket. I knew he was dead. So I left him there, he stayed in my pocket nearly a week. He was my security the only thing I knew. Eventually I couldn't stand the stink so I threw my father's favourite bird off London Bridge. It had to be London Bridge. As it fell, it picked up speed and splashed into the water below.

I never did send that bird back with any note. I always imagined my father coming home from work, looking up into the sky, to see if there was a pigeon bringing back a note from his son.

I swore that day looking off that bridge, that anything I ever had from that day would be looked after proper and buried right.

I stop reading.

There's a picture under the writing. A pigeon sitting on a grapefruit with the word 'sorry' on its leg, where it's tag should be.

Glad's crying, I don't turn round. I look at the bird, I look at the cross and can see Grandad eating a grapefruit. Bert's writing looks good on the wall. Magnificent. I hope I read it well. Maybe I should read it again? I don't know.

Glad doesn't say anything.

"You read that well," Gary says. He's got a tear in his eye. "I never knew that story," he says. Nor did I.

We're brought back to normality with grunts and what sounds like a squeaking bed, it's getting louder. I look up, then at Glad. The music starts again.

"What do you think they're doing, Gary?"

Glad's not looking, so Gary grinds his hips.

"Yeah, that's what I thought," I say. "You been doing any of that?"

"Not nearly enough," he says, shaking his head, smiling, then giving his little laugh. Waiting for me to smile back. But I'm not going to do that.

Nan's got her eyes shut, arms drawn.

"You OK Nan?"

"Yeah, just give me some time."

So we give her some time.

Maybe Glad's right, not liking the woman with the big bottom who lives up on top.

Nan points at me then the ceiling above.

"What?" What's she going to say this time.

"That's that mule and her donkey," she says with tears in her eyes.

"So how many walls did he write on?" I don't want to talk about the mule. I imagine Grandad sitting in darkness in a string vest. Writing down all he could, before Alzheimer's came and took it all away.

I stand looking at his writing.

Glad says, "I've got no idea, but you know what Bert was like when he started something. He never forgave himself for not sending that bird back. Not sending it back with a note. He hadn't spoken about that in years. I'd forgotten."

Nan finishes what she's saying and sits there crying as the bird fades from the wall.

"Can you take a picture of me, by Bert's writing?" Nan asks, still crying.

"I'll give it a go, but I don't know whether it will work. Has your camera got a flash?"

"It's a camera. I don't know what it's got, it's by the phone," Glad says with her eyes shut. Tears rolling down her cheeks. Gary puts his arms round her, I go into the living room, take the camera from its pouch. Nan's phone is one of those old fashioned finger chasers, her address book's open next to that.

The cowboys are still doing whatever they're doing. I walk over to them and turn them off. The room doesn't seem any quieter, just makes the music from above easier to hear. The lights rock. The donkey and the mule are still at it, the banging hasn't stopped.

Was it like that for Gary? Now I'm thinking like Glad. It's been a long day. It's not even come to an end. I'm drunk and I think I'm talking out loud.

The front door bell goes. Loud enough for Glad to hear. It uses two batteries. I put them in for her once, she was amazed I could do it. She didn't have me down as someone who was good with his hands. Two batteries going in a hole and she thought I was good with my hands.

"I'll get it, Nan."

I walk past Gary, Glad still in her chair. I open the door. The horseshoe shakes and the spurs rattle.

Kenny's there smiling, standing next to a man who can see.

I'd forgotten about Kenny.

"Kenny." I hold out my hand.

"Hello Nick, thanks for letting me come." Kenny says with his eyes open wide, his nappy rash eyes, his nodding head. He doesn't hold out his. I've got to go through this blind nonsense again. I wonder who read my number out to him.

"Come in," I say, he takes a step. Then stops, turns to the man and takes a folded note from his pocket, says "Keep the change."

The man takes the note, puts it in his pocket. How many times have I done that?

"Having a party then?" the minicab man says, nodding his head at Gary and Glad. Glad's sitting with her drink and her running drunken eyes. Shit, I really have let her drink too much, myself as well.

"Well have a nice night then," the cab driver says and if he'd been wearing a hat he'd have doffed that. He pats Kenny on the shoulder, turns, walks to his idling car.

"Come in Kenny, watch out, there's a step before the door."

I take his arm, guide him in.

"Glad, this is Kenny."

"Good god, he's blind." That's the first thing she says. She's not one to hold a thought in her head. Glad's looking at Kenny's sore eyes, she even has time to shake her head. Kenny wouldn't have seen that.

Kenny smiles, nods his head, then stops and says.

"I am, I am at that."

"And this is my brother Gary, remember, I told you, he's

sleeping at mine."

"Nice to meet you," he says to the room, looking at no one in particular.

"Well I never, a blind man in my house. It's been years. I've always had a soft spot for blind men, and blacks," Glad says.

"Kenny," I say. "Meet Glad. You might find her rude, you might find her sad, but she's always my Nan and I'm sorry if she gets out of order." And then I remember his story, no next of kin, just him and his eyes. I stare at both of them, I'm happy to have a Nan.

I'm pissed.

Kenny nods his head, stops and says, "Nice to meet you. Can I call you Glad?"

"Call her what you like," Gary says looking at Kenny, looking at his eyes.

"Of course dear, I've been called a silly cow, many a time," Glad says, smiling, still with the tears in her eyes.

The introductions have been done. Now the strange silence.

"Shit. I should have gone with that cab to get some fags," Gary says. Why does he want to run away? As if I don't know.

"I've got some," Kenny says and brings them out, lifts the packet into the air.

"He's got loads," I say. "He's a real smoker, not a ponce like you," I say to Gary.

"What are they?" And Gary looks at the pack.

"Marlborough lights," Kenny says.

"Thanks anyway, but I roll my own," Gary says. "I'll go and get some. Anyone want anything from the shops?"

"No," Glad says, I just shake my head. I know where he's going.

"I might catch him if I'm quick enough," Gary says walking to the door. "You sure no one wants anything?" he says again.

"I'm fine," Kenny says, with his grin, his nodding head.

"You'll catch him, what with all that training you do," I say.

The music above starts to thump again. We all look up. Glad looks at Kenny and says

"I've only ever known one blind man. Only had one other blind man in my house. His name was Ronnie Moor. A nice man who lived with his dog. Did you know him?"

"No, I'm sorry I didn't," Kenny says.

"Why the fuck would he know him, Glad? Not all blind men know each other, it's not as if they're in some sort of club," I say.

"He might have," Glad says.

"What like you know all the old people in Sidcup?" Why have I started? So I try to be nice, and say. "Did he make it to the fridge door Glad? This Ronnie Moor?"

"You'll find him there. Have a look when you get Kenny a drink," Glad says, and I don't know if she's back to being friends with me.

"Yeah, I'll do that."

I guide Kenny around Nan. She's still sitting on her seat, legs open.

I take Kenny into the living room, walking him by his

elbow. I feel like I'm walking a dog.

"Sorry about that," I say in his ear. He's got a cut, red and raised, with a little trickle of blood, behind his ear.

"It's fine," he says.

"You've got a cut."

Kenny takes his hand to his face.

"By your ear," I say, he runs a finger over the cut.

"So then?" I say. And then there's a pause, nothing said. I'm left with looking at him, and he's left smelling me. Because I'm sure by now I stink.

"My wife thinks I'm having an affair," Kenny says. I look at him, he's straight in with it. That's how I should be, enough of this internal shit. People need to be told. Treat them like a punter in the back of the cab.

"She's right, isn't she?" I say. And she is, if yesterday is anything to go by.

"It's not what you think. She thinks it's a woman we used to know."

I don't know what he's talking about, or what to say, so I don't. I just look at him. The blind man standing in the middle of Nan's room, with one hand in his pocket, the other out. He's the same man as yesterday, but his happiness gone.

"Affair, hey?" I say.

"How about that photo, Nick?" Glad shouts from the hall. "You got that camera yet?" She's like a spoiled child, doesn't want to be left on her own for a minute.

"I'm on my way love. She's pretty old, having a rough time," I say, turning to Kenny who's rocking his head. He's like a rooster with bad eyes.

"How old is she?" Kenny says, bringing out a packet of cigarettes. "Do you mind?"

"No, not at all," I say. He puts a cigarette in his mouth, lights it.

"Well, if she's not lying, ninety two. But she lies," I say as I leave the room.

Nan's in the bathroom when I come out. I hadn't expected to see her there.

"You alright love?"

She's looking at the wall. She turns, looks at me, then back to Bert's wall.

"I'll read you some more if you like?"

She doesn't say anything at first then says, "Help me with my dress?"

"What's that?"

The music's blaring out from above, I'm not sure I heard what I heard.

"Can you help me with my dress?"

She did say what I thought she said. Her back's to me, her voice bouncing off the wall.

I touch my face, stroke the stubble on my chin. Look back at her.

"What, you getting ready for bed. I thought you wanted a photo or something?"

"I want a picture of me with Bert's writing on the wall. I want to be remembered. I'm going to do a card for them all to see."

"So what do you want to wear?" I say. She must be pissed, I

know I am.

"I don't want anything on. Help me off with my dress" She says it angrily now.

"Kenny's here Nan. You want me to undress you? In front of Kenny Boy." And why did I call him that?

"He can't see, you fool."

"I know he can't see, but he's got ears. Better than your's or mine."

"Just take the photo, and stop talking. He won't care," Nan says. I don't know whether it's the drink or the day, but something's got into her. She stands with her back to me. A zip ready to be pulled, ready to release her from her dress. I'm not going to do it, I ain't going to pull the zip on my Nan's dress.

"You going to help me or what?" She says.

Still the music comes from above. Nan's hands bent over her back, looking for the tip of the zip. I'm staring at the finger, the zip. I've never been so frightened of a zip before. All I can think of to say is.

"I'm your grandson, Nan." I'm pathetic. I'm not up to this. "Please don't, how about another drink?"

"You can't even undo a zip?" Glad says. Says it in that mocking way. I'll fucking pull your zip, pull it right off your back, what do you want from me? I think.

"It's a tricky one," I say. "It's got a clip, and some sort of clasp. And I'm useless with zips" And I'm not going anywhere near it.

"Just do it, or would you rather I got a professional in? Wasted all that money, on some ponce with a camera." She shakes the back of her head at me. She's waiting and ready. Glad doesn't like to waste money, doesn't like to waste a drop. This is going to be hard to get out of.

"Undo the dress. People will remember me better after I'm gone. I want them to see what I came to."

"What, like a calling card?" I say.

"Whatever's that?"

I'm just about to explain, then I think 'what's the fucking point?'

She's still there with her hand on the zip. I could push her over, but I know I'm not going to do that.

"I used to watch him writing with a whisky in my hand and my slip on. And that's how I want the photo."

I look at Glad. Her and Bert they had a thing going, right to the end.

"Yeah, they'll remember you, and they'll also want to know what perv took the shot. That's going to be me. How am I going to explain that?"

"You can tell them whatever you bloody like. Tell them it's what I asked you to do. Tell them you was doing me a favour. You was being family, you were doing something none of them could do."

"Why don't you get Gary to do it? Don't forget he was your favourite."

"I know that, but he ain't here."

She's right, he's not. I know where he'll be. Getting nice and close to Pam.

"I'm in my thirties Nan, I'm getting a bit old to be told what to do."

"You're still a child, son. You'll always be a child to me."

She looks at me with her ninety-two-year-old eyes. I've got a very long way to go. How many more roundabouts, traffic lights, diversions to go round? How much more traffic must I sit in? Gradually eating me out.

"Shit, Nan. I don't want to do it. That's the end of it," I say.

"Hello?" Kenny says from the other room. Saved by a blind man from another room.

"I'll go and see what he wants." I'm off before Nan can say boo.

I walk out the door, go in to Kenny. He's standing there, he hasn't sat down. I didn't even show him to a seat. He's exactly where I left him, in the middle of the room.

"You reckon you could get us a drink and find an ashtray for this."

He shows me his hand, it's full of ash. Shit, I should have sorted him out better than this. I pick up the coal truck. Look at Bert's last piece of ash, tip it into my pocket, hand Kenny the ashtray.

"This used to be my Grandad's." After I've said it, I wonder why I did. "What do you want to drink?"

"A beer would be good. If you've got one that is?" He smiles at me, then flicks some ash onto the back of the truck.

"Yeah, we've got beer, I'll get you one."

"Here," I say as I take Kenny's elbow, lead him to a chair. He sits down.

"Thanks," he says.

"I should have done it earlier, I'm sorry, there's a lot going on," I say.

"So I hear," Kenny says.

I nod my head, turn and go outside. Glad's starting to lower her dress.

"Just wait Glad, I'll be back," I say with gritted teeth. I'm trying to buy some time. The music from above's still loud. I've got to get Kenny his drink. I've become very busy. I go into the kitchen open the memorial fridge. Rows and rows of dead names. I could be staring into a graveyard, but I'm not, because it's a fridge. I shake my head.

"What was the name of that guy you said?" I shout.

"Who?" Glad shouts back.

"The blind man, the one you knew?"

"Ronnie Moor. Nicest blind fella I've ever met."

"Ronnie Moor. That's it," I say, scanning the names on the door.

"Yeah, he's here, he's made it onto the door. Do you want to know who he's sandwiched between?" I shout back.

"I don't give a damn," Glad shouts. "If you die before me, you'll be there." Then she goes quiet. I close the fridge door.

I walk out of the kitchen with its painted white walls, Grandad's writing on top. Glad's out of her dress now, standing in her slip. She's done it all on her own.

"So you managed it then?"

"No thanks to you," she says back.

I walk past her, take the beer into Kenny who's quiet on the seat, a cigarette hanging from his mouth.

"Thanks," he says, as I put the can in his hand. "And thanks for letting me come round." I look at him.

"That's alright," I say. And it is. I want to talk to him about Gary, Pam. God, do I want to talk.

"Nick," Glad shouts. She wants me back. I haven't got time to talk, Kenny Boy.

"Alright, Nan, be back in a minute Kenny."

Glad's sitting there, on a chair in her slip. Gold on her fingers, gold round her neck. Her eyes are closed, her skin sore. I'm looking at her now, like never before. I've never really checked her out.

"Look love, I'm going to ask them to turn the music down. The light in the living room's swinging."

"Whatever you want," Glad says. It's as if she's forgotten, doesn't care, why she's sitting in her slip on the chair, in the middle of the hall.

I turn and as I do, Glad says, "Her." It makes me jump.

I look at Glad. She points to the ceiling. I know who she means now.

"Her up top, she takes this trampoline outside, bounces on it, sort of thing. Up and down, everything swinging, everyone can see. She knows people in the block watch. What else we got to do? One time, she gave me and Bert this wave. We didn't wave back, that was bad for Bert. He wouldn't have liked not waving back. Lord only knows who she thinks she is."

I think she's stopped talking, but she hasn't.

"Her Dad, he was a lovely man. I used to take him food up on a plate. He always thanked me."

"Look Nan, go in and sit with Kenny. I'll go and get her to turn the music down, this is a joke. Come on."

I hold out my hand, she puts out hers, I pull her to her feet. Her breathing's deep, heavy, she's looking like every year she's lived.

I take Glad into Kenny, he's sitting there with his beer and another fag hanging from his lip, with Bert's ashtray on his lap. The coal sack's filling up with ash.

"Here Nan, sit by the fire."

I've got a blind man and an old woman in her slip. That won't be bothering Kenny, what with him being blind. And Glad? She's too sad to care. She must be pissed. I've got to get that pill in her glass. I go outside, get my shoes.

"You'll be alright won't you, you two?" I say as I come back into the room.

They're already talking, Glad with her whisky, Kenny with his beer.

"So what's it like being blind, Kenny?" Glad asks.

Kenny says, "I'll tell you if you tell me what it's like being old?"

Glad laughs. "That's easy, just waiting for the end to come. The last sunset to be seen."

Kenny can't see the tears in her eyes, the dying skin. He's saved. And at this very moment he's lucky to be blind.

Kenny turns to me with his rocking head, and says, "We'll be fine, won't we Glad?"

"Course we will. And him, he's nothing but a fool," she says looking at me.

"Alright, up I go to sort out the woman with the arse, ay Glad?"

I am, I don't know what I'm going to say but I'll say

something.

"That's my boy." She laughs. Kenny looks at Nan.

"Nan, tell Kenny about the woman with the arse."
Glad looks at me.

"I'll bloody do that," she says and she will. She uncrosses her legs and leans forward in her chair, I can smell her from here.

Chapter 18

I open the front door, and leave. The horseshoe shakes, the spurs rattle. I wait until they've stopped. Then I wait some more.

I climb the lino steps, every one a squeaker. I get to the arse's door. I don't know why I'm thinking like that. I wait at the door. There's a picture of a dog with a sign under it.

'Guard dog on parole.'

"What?" I'm pissed. It doesn't say that. I read it wrong.

'Guard dog on patrol.' That's what it says. The other way's meaner, I wouldn't go in a flat with a guard dog on parole. What's it fucking done? How many years did it get? And why's it out?

I flap the bronze flap. Do it again, wait by the door. And move back, just in case that dog's in there.

A bolt is slid, a chain lifted and dropped. I don't hear a dog, but I smell a woman coming to the door.

The door opens.

"Yes, can I help you?"

She's wearing a Chinese silk robe with a tie around her waist. I smile, I know what she's been doing. And then I start to think of Pam and Gary. That's where I should be now, putting my size eleven boot in. Then I remember why I'm staring at this woman in a robe.

"Yeah, hello I'm looking after my Nan tonight, and well, we were wondering whether you'd mind turning down the music, please?" I'm happy with myself for remembering to say please.

She looks at me.

"Oh I'm sorry, is it too loud? It's my birthday," she says. Says it quickly, says it like she's embarrassed.

"Happy Birthday," I say back.

"Thanks."

She looks at me. She's attractive, a bit younger than me but still attractive.

"How old are you then?"

"You should never ask a woman her age. It's one of the first rules."

"Sorry, you're right. I've been drinking." I smile at her.

"I can smell that." She pauses, "Thirty six, I don't know why I'm celebrating." She says it with a smile. She's not cross. I take a step back.

"You've still got a long way to go. Happy Birthday," I say again.

Rod Stewart singing again. You either like him or you don't.

"Have you got him on loop? You know he won't sing that anymore, not live anyway."

The woman in the Chinese robe looks at me. "Who won't sing what?"

"Old Rodney Boy, Rod Stewart, he won't sing 'Do you think I'm sexy' any more. Not live anyway."

"And why's that?" She looks at me, she's got good eyes. I don't want her to think I'm flirting, so I look away and say.

"In case someone shouts, 'No.' I read it somewhere. He's worried about his hair, his size, everything really."

"Is that so?" She laughs.

"He's over sixty now. Eight wives, maybe nine, since I've been here."

She smiles. "Are you a fan?"

"No, but I've been listening to him all night. He's OK." I say, putting myself in it, trying to get myself out.

"You seem to know all about him."

"My Mum gets *Hello*."

"You're a bit old to be living with your Mum." And she laughs.

"I don't live with her, I read it when I go round. In the toilet." Why did I tell her that?

"Oh, really," she says, then we go silent. Look at each other.

"So, you are?" she says.

"I'm Nick, Glad's grandson."

"I'm Elizabeth." She stops talking, then goes on. "I don't think your Gran likes me very much."

You're fucking right about that.

"Sure she does," I say. "Well, she's not said anything to me." And it's poker eye time. I hope Dad taught me well.

Elizabeth looks, smiles. She has a hand on the door, and a knee pointing at me. Behind her are two fluorescent coats on hangers. With St John's Ambulance in silver on the back.

"So you're in the St John's then?" I say, nodding to the coats behind her back. She turns.

"Yeah, I've been with them for a good few years."

"Any good? I've always wondered who did that sort of thing." I nod to the coats again.

I have, I've always thought you must be bloody odd. Odd or good, one of the two, maybe a bit of both.

"We enjoy it," she says.

And then we have a quiet moment. I don't know what to say, nor does she. So I move my feet, look up, and smile.

"Do you get paid, you know, doing the St John's thing?"

"No, it's all voluntary."

I keep looking at the coats. "It's all voluntary." I repeat what she just said. Why would anyone want to do that? Then I say, "It's good that people like you exist."

She laughs.

"I'm sorry about the music, it's very insensitive of me. What with the funeral being today. I'll turn it right down."

I'm looking at Elizabeth thinking that Glad's got her all wrong.

"Happy Birthday again," I say.

"Thanks," she says.

"I've got a friend downstairs who's birthday was yesterday. Same zodiac sign. You'd probably get on."

"That's not always the case." She laughs. I don't know why I'm talking zodiacs. I'm not interested in them. I'm just talking now, babbling. So I stop. She looks at me for a while then says.

"I'll turn the music down, I'm sorry we've had it so loud. We were dancing. She doesn't sleep, your Nan."

"I wouldn't know about that." I'm lying, I slept with her last night, her tossing and wailing, screams in her sleep.

"She doesn't, I used to hear them at night, talking or watching TV," Elizabeth says.

"I'm sorry, she's a bit deaf. Hard of hearing, deaf as a door nail really. She loves her cowboys, bang, bang, that sort of stuff," I say.

"Yeah. We've got used to it now. It's like living on top of the OK Corral." She smiles. "You don't look like her, your Nan that is."

"I'm younger."

"I can see that," she says. Then a man comes to the door, in his pants and a string vest.

"Anything the matter?" he says looking at me, says it in a friendly way. I smile, raise a hand. He raises one back. He's got a big round face. He looks like a St John's man, I think as I look at him. He'd look the part in his coat. You'd trust him if he leaned over you, and said "Are you alright?"

Elizabeth turns, says to him. "Can you turn the music down love?"

"Sure," he says turning, in his pants.

"He seems nice," I say. He does.

"He is," she says.

Glad's reading them all wrong, maybe Mum's right, we should get her in a home, get her in one quick. Mum thinks Glad's going nuts. I haven't seen her enough, she's always been pretty strange.

"So you're both in the St John's then?"

"Yeah, we met there, eight years ago. Met at Diana's funeral. We got told off for talking so much. We just couldn't stop talking. We just clicked. He was the first man I'd clicked with in years." She smiles and shakes her head at the same time.

"So why not join the real ambulance brigade?"

"I never got in. I wanted to, I just never got in."

"Oh, I'm sorry," I say.

"Give your Gran my condolences, I'm sorry about Bert. I really am. It was last week wasn't it?"

"Yeah, I can't even remember what day."

"I remember the night. She cried, wailed all night. I would have gone down, but she wouldn't have opened the door. We called the ambulance though." She stops talking. I look at her waist.

"Thanks for doing that. Thanks a lot," I say.

"I just wish we could have done more."

"It's OK, he died in his sleep, smoking."

"Smoking, he could have burnt us down." She smiles. "Say sorry to your Gran, I mean that."

I nod my head. She closes the door.

The woman meant it, she was sorry about Glad. And she only bounces on her trampoline to keep fit, but I can't tell Nan that. She wouldn't believe me anyway.

I walk back down the squeaking stairs. Back to Kenny and Nan.

Chapter 19

"The man's back," I say as I walk in. And there they are. Glad and Kenny. "I'm back," I say it louder this time.

Glad's sitting there. Her breasts are out. Uncovered, drooping towards the floor. How the fuck did they get out? Glad's got her tits out and what am I supposed to do?

Kenny's holding the camera, the lens is looking at Glad. He's a metre away, with a big smile. He's in darkness, he can't see a thing.

"Hello?" I say again, louder this time.

"Alright?" Kenny says turning towards me and the door.

"What's going on?" I don't want to look at Nan, but she's got this grin and the gold round her neck is shining. So I do look.

"Anything the matter?" Kenny says. "You have trouble with that neighbour?" he says.

"No, no trouble with her," I say. He doesn't know. Glad's still got this strange grin. It's a cross between a stroke and a smile.

"He's never used a camera before," Glad says. "I'm teaching him how."

"Oh, is that so. That's very good of you Glad," I say. "Getting the hang of it Kenny? She a good teacher, my Nan?"

I put my hand in my pocket, feel the pill, I'm going to run over and shove it down her throat.

Kenny says. "Glad just said to point it at her voice. Pretty easy really. I've never used one before. I'm going to take one of Lizzie when I go home." Kenny's smiling, he's happy, he's found something new to do.

"That'll be nice Kenny. Are you done Glad, has he taken enough?"

She sits, looking at me, there's a lot of flesh.

"He's only taken one," Glad says.

"Well, how many do you want?" I need another drink, but I'm not going to get Glad one. No way.

Glad looks at me, doesn't say a word for a while, and I look. Then she says, "I'm having my picture taken, what do you think?"

"Yeah, I can see that. But what about your?" I lift my top up, bounce my breasts around.

Glad laughs. My hoops are showing, they're still sore.

"He can't see, he's blind, you fool," she says shaking her head, gold bouncing between the parting of the waves.

I look at her, then look at him.

"You're right, but I can, so there's a slight problem, if you don't mind Nan, cover up."

"Don't you worry about that, what you can or can't see. Isn't that right Kenny?" Glad says, she still hasn't pulled her slip up. And Kenny's become her best mate. "Kenny and me have been talking," Glad says. "He's a really nice boy."

"She's great, your Nan." Kenny's smiling, rocking. Well what else would he be doing.

"Don't believe anything she says," I say. "She'll put you in her web, and I tell you, it's fucking hard to break free."

The doorbell goes, it better be Gary, he can sort this out. He's older, more like Nan, and as Nan said, he was her pet.

"Who's that?" Glad says.

"It'll be Gary. Pull your slip up"

But she doesn't, just gives me this fake grin. I take my eyes off her, move to the door and open it wide.

"Hello."

It isn't Gary. It's the woman from up top. Smiling. So I smile.

"I thought if your Nan couldn't sleep, she could have a cup of valerian tea."

"Tea?" I say.

"Who is it?" Nan shouts from behind me.

I close my eyes, open them, she's still there.

"Um, thanks, she's more of a whisky girl. But I'll see if she wants some." I take the cup of tea, but I'm not going to let her in. I keep a foot on the door. There's no way she's coming in.

"Who is it?" Nan shouts again.

"What's you're name again?" I whisper. I've forgotten. I'm starting to sweat.

"Elizabeth" She mouths it softly.

"Elizabeth," I say.

"Who?" Nan says.

I raise my eyebrows, "It doesn't matter Glad," and shake my head. Elizabeth smiles at me, again I smile back.

"I don't know no Elizabeth, tell her to come in."

Glad's moving off her chair behind my back. Puffing, panting, pulling herself up. I can hear it all, I'm not even looking at her. But I know what she's doing. I turn, she's on her feet, starting to walk to the door. Oh fuck, her balance has gone. I can see from here. She's pissed, she's going to fall. I run towards her, catch her before she goes down. But I can't take her weight, we both slide to the floor. I hit my head on hers as we go down. She comes to a stop on top of me. All over me, old folds and sores. Her dead old weight. I've never been so close. Her skin's covered in a rash. I've got a breast in my face and I'm finding it hard to breathe, I push away, come out into light.

The door swings open, Elizabeth sees what she sees. She stands by the door looking in. There's one thing I can do, and I'm going to do it fast. I smile.

"Hello," I say. And smile from under Glad.

She's staring at us, in her fluffy mules.

I move from under Glad's other breast. Smile once more, if in doubt, smile.

"Give us a hand, would you?" I say. "I can't move her, I'm fucking stuck actually." I'm all tucked under Glad.

Elizabeth moves from the door, comes in with her fluffy feet. Looks at us, not a smile in sight. Then turns and sees Kenny. He's still holding the camera, rocking his head. God what must she think. Kenny doesn't care, he takes another shot, and another, he's on a roll. The shutter goes then the flash. I'm going to be in quite a few, me with naked Nan lying on top. That'll look good in the family album. Look, here's me with Glad. And Lucy will say. "Why's she got nothing on?" How am I going to explain that?

"Get her out, get that whore away," Nan shouts. She's just seen who it is. The devil from up top.

"Look, how are we going to get up?" I say, shaking my head. "Stop shouting."

"I don't want her to touch me. I've never shouted in my life."

"You just did again," I say.

"No I never." She starts to push away at Elizabeth.

"It's all too late for fucking that, behave yourself," I say.

"Kenny, come here and help," Glad shouts to Kenny, who's still holding the camera, but not taking shots.

"Kenny can't see," I say.

"I know that, he's got arms ain't he, he's not a cripple?" Glad's talking about him as if he isn't there. And so am I.

I slide out from under her bulk, rise to my feet, look at Glad on the floor. She's a big woman, knackered, bloated, sore on life.

I bend down. "Come on." I put my hand under her arm. It's damp, hairy, and not a place I want it to be.

"Get her away, don't let that whore touch me," Glad shouts.

"You've already said that," I say, my eyes bearing down on her, Glad stares back.

Elizabeth's looking at Kenny, and I can't believe it, she's not even interested in us anymore.

"See, she's already got the eye for Kenny," Glad says.

"Excuse me, Elizabeth, give us a hand?" I say, she stops looking at Kenny, puts an arm under Glad.

"Get her off." And Glad's pushing away with her arms. I tap Glad's hand.

"Now, you be good," I say looking at Glad. "On the count of three. One two three, lift." Glad's still trying to push Elizabeth's hands away.

Slowly she begins to rise. She's as heavy as all the potatoes she used to hump from a lorry. Heavy, full with dead beaten life.

We haul her to her feet, slowly move her to the chair. She's no cat. She pants, she's breathing hard, going grey in the face. Her head falls forward, I'm left looking at her deep craggy neck.

Elizabeth's got tears in her eyes. She's crying over Nan, and Glad's calling her a whore. Well I never.

"You alright Glad?" I say, but she doesn't look up. I don't even know if she can hear me. "Thanks for that," I say turning to Elizabeth. Elizabeth's not looking at me she's back looking at Kenny. She's got a thing going with Kenny already. Glad's right?

"He's blind, you know that?" I say.

"Oh I know." And still she doesn't turn. "Do you want some help getting her into bed?" She pauses, then "I think she should lie down." And the whole time she doesn't take her eyes off Kenny.

"Yeah. Glad, we're going to get you into bed." I can't see her face, but I hear a little voice say.

"OK." She's surrendered. Thank fuck.

We've got to get her to bed before she dies. She could at any moment. I don't want to be clearing up that mess. A bottle of scotch coming out of her stomach, hitting the floor. A blind man and a woman, my witness.

"Kenny, use that bloody camera," Nan says, her head leaning forward, eyes looking at the floor. She's woken from the grave. And there's no surrender yet. She's back.

"Not now. Tomorrow," I say. "Jesus Christ, what's going on Glad?"

"Who says there's a tomorrow? And who are you to tell me what to do?" Glad says, lifts her head up, now she's facing the room, with her wet, tired eyes. "Anyway, I look better at night, a regular English rose," She laughs. Gives Elizabeth her fake smile. "Go on, have a good look. Look at me, you whore." Glad's still got anger on her tongue. "Have a good look love, see what you'll become," She says.

She doesn't give a fuck. She never has, I mean she really doesn't. She's got fuel in her. Poison more like, I think, as I stare.

"I'm sorry," I say turning to Elizabeth. "I'm sure she likes you. It's the funeral, Bert dying, the whisky, er, what else could it be?" I rock my head, and I'm doing a good impersonation of Kenny.

Elizabeth says to Glad, "I don't know why you hate me so much, but I know you always have."

"You don't know?" Glad tuts. "Leaving your Dad to rot and die? You don't know?" She says again with her face screwed tight. Every line in her face she's ever grown, showing.

"You don't understand, I didn't even know he was ill, he wouldn't speak to me. He hadn't spoken to me for years, we'd had a row," Elizabeth says.

"Oh, you had a row," and Glad says it, taking the piss out of the way Elizabeth talks. "Ah, but he was good enough for you to have his flat. Came running from under your rock for that. He was a good man, your Dad. He worked with all those kids. And his own daughter wouldn't give him a hand. Left him to rot. Look at my Grandson, he's here." Glad shakes her head, then looks down at the floor.

"I'm fucking here alright. Can't say I want to be, right this minute," I say and close my eyes, it's no better there. I open them and look at Kenny, he doesn't know what to do. He's still rocking, looking high into the air, pulling a cigarette from his pocket. And he thought his place was going to be rocky tonight. He's left a storm, for a hurricane.

"I'll get you a cover, Glad, you've got goose pimples all over you," I say.

I walk past Kenny, touch his arm. "What a fucking night. You'll remember this, won't you? And you thought you had it bad, hey?" I say.

Kenny nods, but he's not nodding at me. He's got his slits fixed on Elizabeth now.

I leave them all to it. I've got to get into Glad's room for a bit of peace. I look at the bed, I want to get under it. I could. Who'd find me? I get on my knees, put my head under. But I won't fit, there's a suitcase full of dust in the way. Fuck.

I pull the bedspread from the sheets, there's a photo on the bed. A photo on the bed, what a surprise. Am I pissed? Is this going on?

Grandad, nothing on, naked, just him in a police hat. Glad's sleeping with a picture of her man. Even in death Glad wants to be close to Bert. I look at the picture, I never saw him like this. He was in good shape.

"You penny grabbing whore. Nothing but a mule, being humped by a donkey."

Glad's off.

"Hey, hey," I shout from the room, dropping the picture to the bed. I don't want to go back in, but I'm not going to let Glad talk to Elizabeth like that. I get off my knees, back to my feet. Pray, that's what I need to do, say a little prayer.

"I beg your pardon," Elizabeth says, as I go back into the hall. She's quite posh this Elizabeth, well spoken. I walk past Kenny.

"You put this on, and don't be so fucking rude," I say, walking to Nan with the cover in my hand.

"I'm sorry. She's got a way with words, haven't you Glad?" I shout, making sure she can hear. Glad's looking at me like

205

I'm a traitor, someone's who's stabbed her in the back. I check behind her ear, she's on the right setting.

"You're nothing but a coward, I thought you'd stand by me," Glad says shaking her head at me. "Coward, always have been, always will be. Letting that whore touch me."

She's called me that ever since the time she saw me being bullied. I wouldn't fight back. He was big, I couldn't fight back. Glad came over and knocked him out.

Elizabeth says, "Let's get her to bed, she looks tired."

I nod my head. I'm glad I've got the ambulance crew here. Glad's got a cut above her eye and blood's starting to drip down. So now I've got Kenny and Glad with blood wounds. That doesn't leave many of us left.

"Come on, Glad." I take Glad's arm.

"I don't want you to touch me again. Leaving your Dad, like you did. Leaving him to die alone. You should be ashamed of yourself. I won't have no heartless whore touching my arm." Glad moves her arm away from me. And she's off again.

"It's me, Nick," I say. She doesn't even know who I am now.

"I know who you are, it's her I was talking to," she says.

"Well, why look at me? And anyway, you've already said your party piece. It's time to go to bed. Come on, and have a couple of these?" I get the sleeping tablets out of my pocket, hold them in my hand.

"Elizabeth?" Kenny says.

I turn, look at Kenny, it's the way he said it. Like a squeak, he doesn't speak with a squeak. Kenny's got tears running down his cheeks. He's crying now. He's fallen for Elizabeth pretty quick.

"Look, if you're all going to cry, I am too. Come on, let's pull ourselves together. Sort this shit out." And who the hell am I talking to. I'm doing a rallying call for myself.

Elizabeth turns to Kenny. "Kenny? Kenny is that you?" And now she's crying.

I look at them, Kenny's nappy rash eyes haven't moved from Elizabeth. Elizabeth walks over to Kenny. I bring my hand to my face, cover my eyes.

"Kenny, it really is you," she says.

"Yeah, it's him." I butt in. "So you know him then?" I say.

"How can they? he's blind, you fool. She's nothing but a whore, they've only just met. Two minutes, no more than that, and she already wants to grind her hips, look at her, she's even getting ready to kiss him," Glad says, from her chair. "See I told you, nothing but a whore. Look at her flirting with poor Kenny, he can't even see." And she's nodding again, she's had all the proof she needs, to know what Elizabeth's all about.

I look at Glad, she's nodding, nodding her head. She could be right? She can't be. What am I, going fucking mad? Fuck this.

"Glad, shut up," I say. I don't know why I picked on her, it could have been anyone in the room.

"Elizabeth?"

"Yes, it's me Kenny." And Elizabeth uses a finger to wipe away one of Kenny's tears. She runs a finger down to his lips.

Fast mover. Fuck, I'm thinking like Glad. I really am, I'm out of the same mould.

Kenny stretches out a hand, Elizabeth takes it.

"Now look at her" Glad says, from her grandstand seat.

Elizabeth's not listening to Glad, she's all over Kenny.

"It's me," she says again. And its like watching Dr. Zhivago, the scene at the station, when they're hugging and kissing and it all goes white. I think it was that film.

I let myself slide down the wall, until my bum hits the floor. I'm tired, I'm pissed, not up for any of this.

They're touching each other's faces, crying, holding each other. And now they're kissing, I don't believe this. I start to laugh. I'm laughing in the corner of the room.

"See, see," Glad says to anyone who will listen. But I'm still laughing.

I don't know what to do. So I sit and laugh. It's been a long day, I never thought it would come to two strangers kissing in front of Nan.

They stop kissing, Elizabeth holds Kenny's chin. I look at Glad, and I know what she's getting ready to do.

"So, you know each other then, or is this love at first sight?" It's all I can think of to say.

"Elizabeth is the girl I was telling you about yesterday. I can't believe it, you know, the warden's daughter," Kenny says as if I should know.

"Warden's daughter?" I don't know what he's talking about.

"From the children's home, I told you, yesterday in the pub. She played the violin, we used to meet on a Wednesday, until her Dad caught us," Kenny says rocking, with a smile on his face. He's so happy.

"Thursdays," Elizabeth says.

And now I know. The warden's daughter, the violin player, the candle blower. I look at Elizabeth in a different light now. Now I understand.

"Sorry, Thursdays," Kenny says. And they both laugh. "How many years has it been?"

"Too many," Elizabeth says. " Where did they all go?"

"See, see, nothing but a whore. What's she done to you Kenny?" Glad says nodding her head, in total agreement with herself. "He was such a nice boy til she got here," she says to anyone who will listen, and I guess that's me.

"Yeah, yeah, we all know what you think Glad," I say. "Look, let's get you to bed." She's there with a blanket round her shoulders, and a breast hanging out. I push myself off the floor, get back to my feet.

But Kenny and Elizabeth, they're not bothered with us anymore. A whole new chapter's opened up for them.

"I always looked, you know that? I always looked for you," Kenny says. "Even after I left the home."

"How could he look, he's blind?" Glad cuts in.

"Oh Kenny," Elizabeth says.

Kenny laughs. "I even called my daughter after you. You meant a lot to me, you know that?"

Elizabeth's shaking her head. "You called your daughter after me? Oh Kenny." And they kiss again, holding their lips together, all I can do is watch. I shouldn't be here listening to this. Or watching come to think of it.

Glad's off again. "Look at her, the whore. Look at her go." I walk over to Glad.

"Glad, open your mouth?" I say it softly, I don't want to worry her, but I know exactly what I'm going to do.

"What?"

I put my hand on her lips, prise her mouth open. Push the

sleeping pills in. "Swallow them," I shout. "Swallow the fucking pills."

I don't know what she's saying, but she's saying something. It sounds like she can't breathe.

"Have you swallowed them?" She nods her head. "Good, now be a good girl." I take my hands from Glad's mouth.

"Nothing but a whore," she says, with bits of pill spraying out. I give up.

"Kenny, tell Glad here about Elizabeth's Dad? Tell her what a lovely man he was."

"I'd rather not," he says shaking. "Do you still play that violin?" Kenny says looking to the ceiling.

"Oh, she plays it, you should hear the racket," Glad says.

"Glad," I say. I'm waiting now, waiting for those pills to take her under. I'm watching her when the doorbell goes.

I look at the door, then at the others, they're all looking at the door.

"Now, who the fuck's that? Shall I see?" I say, in the most sarcastic voice I can muster. "Want anymore guests Glad, expecting anyone?" I shout. God I've been doing some shouting today. I don't give her time to answer, just move my arse to the door.

"Now then, let's see who it is?" I turn and smile once more to the room.

It's got to be Gary. It is him, with a fag in his hand.

"Alright?" he says, and moves an eyebrow as he says it.

"Yeah, come in, come on." And with my hand I gesture to the room.

"Tada," I say, if I had a trumpet I'd be blowing that as well.

Gary sees the crowd in the hall. Glad's looking at him. Her breast swings free, I'm used to that now, it ain't bothering me.

"Good god," he says.

"You'll get used to it Gary." I know what he's seen.

"What the fuck's going on Nick?" he says to me, then to Glad "What you doing love?"

"Just get in and shut the door," I say.

That's it, I don't want anyone else in here. Gary's going to be the last person coming into this room.

Elizabeth and Kenny are holding hands, they look sweet. They could be in love.

"What's happened Glad?" He walks over, says it all nice and softly. You can tell he hasn't been in the room. He's not up to speed. He'll get there.

"She's not dressed, and what's all this stuff around her mouth?"

"He made me do it," Glad says looking at me, sounding like a robot.

"What? He made you undress? Why?"

"No, he made me take them pills," Glad says, taking Gary's hand. "I'm so glad you're back Gary, you don't know what's going on. And poor Kenny over there, look at him, look what she's done."

I'm going to try and clear it all up for Gary. "Look, I've just pushed some sleeping pills down her throat. She should be in bed anyway," I say.

"Why did you do that?" He says, his mouth's open, he's no idea.

I'm fed up with talking to him. Who does he think he is? He thinks I'm a fucking cunt.

"Where you been? Away long enough for a fuck, I'd say. Been fucking, Gary?" I move against the wall, push my hips into it. "Like this was it?" And I show him what I think he's been doing. Moving my penis against the wall.

I shout. "Was she good? Did she holler like a pig?"

Gary looks at me, he thinks I've gone fucking mad, it's in his eyes, maybe I have. I go mad in the cab, why not here?

He's taken a taxi for a fuck with my Pam. Pam against a wall. My little Lucy asleep in bed, hearing them in her dreams. I see it all.

I kiss the wall, pout my lips and walk over to Gary, "That's better," I say and then. "You're a bastard Gary."

I hit him. He stumbles back, I hit him again, then again. Follow that up with a head butt between the eyes. My head splits his skin. And down he goes, on top of Glad, spouting blood.

"Your favourite grandson," I say, as he lands in her lap.

I turn round, walk past Kenny and Elizabeth, they've stopped talking now. I seemed to have got their attention.

"Carry on," I say. "Don't worry about me. Everything's fine. I've been wanting to do that for a while."

"Look what that woman's done to Kenny." It's Glad talking to Gary.

"What woman?" Gary says, wiping his nose.

"The mule." Glad nods her head at the ceiling. "Look what she's doing to poor Kenny." I don't even think she knows what I've just done. She's only got eyes for the 'whore'.

"What, that's not his wife?" Gary says

"No, it's her, the mule," Glad says with a rasp in her throat.

Gary's eyes are swelling, his nose looks broken from here.

And from the bathroom door, Bert's writing is on the wall. What did it say?

I'm not a believer, I don't believe.

"You've broken my fucking nose," Gary says. I stand by Glad's bedroom door, nod my head and go in.

Bert's picture's on the bed. I pick it up. Let myself fall to the pillow. It's been a hell of a day. The picture's in my hand. I stare at it, what's with Albert and Glad and nudity? Then my phone goes. I pull it out of my pocket, bring it to my ear.

It's Pam. My lovely wet Pam.

"How's everything? You got Glad to sleep yet?" she says.

"No, not yet. She's in the hall giving milk to Gary." I laugh.

"Gary doesn't drink milk," Pam says.

"Well he is now. He's back on the breast. Breast is best," I say.

"You're drunk." Pam's annoyed, it's in her voice.

"He's taking milk from Glad, right now. Right this minute he's on the breast," I say again. I can see him, he still on Glad's lap.

"Yeah right, well do you need anything?" Pam says.

There's a pause, then a sigh from Pam. While she's sighing, I stare at Grandad's picture. I turn it, to the cardboard back. Grandad's signed it, he would, wouldn't he. It says *to Frankie*. Now who's Frankie? I close my eyes. And then I remember, Kissing Frankie Knight, well I never. Grandad had a thing going with Frankie.

"What's that?" Pam says, I must have said it out loud.

"It looks like I slept with Bert last night" I say, turning the picture in my hand.

"What?" Pam says.

"Grandad, I slept with a picture of him last night, me and Glad must have been tucked in with him." But I haven't finished yet. "Who did you sleep with Pam?"

Pam's not going to answer that. "Look love, I've got something to tell you." There's silence, a long silence. I don't like silences on a phone.

"I'm listening," I say, and I am, but all there is, is silence.

Pam says, in a soft voice. "There never seems to be the right time to tell you." And she pauses, I wait. "I can't seem to talk to you anymore," she says.

"No, you fucking can't, can you?" I say. I know what's coming. My legs are shaking.

And still she's silent. So I wait, with Grandad looking up at me.

"I'm two months pregnant, love. It's back to nappies, and sleepless nights," she says.

"Is it mine?" I say in a slow, deep voice, shaking on the bed.

"Of course it is, you silly fool"

Gary comes to the door, holding Glad's hand. He's covered in blood and Glad's got her breasts out.